ISABELLA WELLS

# THE KINGDOM SHE LOST

### A NOVEL

BOOK ONE
THE ATALIAN CHRONICLES

The Kingdom She Lost

Copyright © 2024 Isabella Wells

All rights reserved.

No part of this publication may be reproduced, distributed, or transmitted in any form or by any means, including photocopying, recording, or other electronic or mechanical methods, without the prior written permission of the publisher, except as permitted by U.S. copyright law. For permission requests, contact isabellawauthor@gmail.com

The story, all names, characters, and incidents portrayed in this production are fictitious. No identification with actual persons (living or deceased), places, buildings, and products is intended or should be inferred.

Paperback ISBN: 979-8-9900132-0-9 EBook ISBN: 979-8-9900132-1-6 Hardcover ISBN: 979-8-9900132-2-3

Book cover, chapter drawings, and map design by Isabella Wells

Edited by Andrea Martinez-Wells

Formatted using Atticus

First edition 2024

*For my sister who I named Safiya after.*

*You have a flame inside of you that shouldn't be hidden from the world. Find your inner courage and bravery to tackle your doubts and fears.*

*Never let the words and actions of others belittle you. I want this series to remind you that challenges are there to help you overcome them so that you can find the light and get stronger every time.*

***Stronger every time.***

*This is for you.*

# PLAYLIST

"IN YOUR EYES" BY PETER GABRIEL
"CALEDONIA" BY CELTIC WOMAN
"IF THIS IS THE END (THE SOUND OF
BELIEF)" BY GREEK FIRE
"WHO AM I" BY ENZO INGROSSO FT
CONRAD SEWELL
"LONG LIVE (TAYLOR'S VERSION)" BY
TAYLOR SWIFT
"THE SECRET CAVE" BY JOE HISAISHI
"DIE YOUNG" BY SHEPPARD
"VIVA LA VICTORIA" BY ECLIPSE
"THE HIDDEN WORLD" BY JOHN
POWEL AND JÓNSI
"UNBREAKABLE" BY KEIINO

QUE ISLANDS

ORSA SLOPES

FYRE

LUDORA

THE WASTELANDS

ATALA

GREAT SILVA FOREST

DEVAL

CRASMERE

QUEENSIDE

LILIANE

EVERGREEN PLAINS

WESTERN DESERT

MISRAHI

AL KURMA

ENDRANCIA

MIRAGE DELTA

THE OCEAN ABYSS

N
E
S
W

Content Warnings

This book contains and mentions depictions of war, violence, blood, and torture.

*"Like many stories in our world, this one starts with a girl. A girl not knowing what she had in store but pursuing it with courage and kindness to her fellow countrymen. Nevertheless, it's also about a boy fighting to keep the ones he loves close and finding himself along the way.*

*And this is only just the beginning..."*

*The Royal Atalian Chronicles- Vol 10, Book 1 Recounting the events between the years of 203 and 250, 200 years after the death of Aila Dawn, the first King of Atalia.*

# PART ONE
## THE RETIRED SOLDIER

# CHAPTER 1

*"A woman! A girl! Running through the forest. She's frantically running away from something! You have to help her!"*

Flying out from the leaves of the trees, a burgundy-red feathered falcon flew into view. Isa turned surprised as Ayden flew above her head.

"Lead me to her. Show me the way, show me where she is," Isa asked her falcon companion, packing up the rest of the carcasses.

Making sure her bow was strapped tight and her bag secure, Isa jumped into a run stepping past branches and over tree trunks ever so silently. Isa knew every corner of the forest having grown up in the area.

The sound of panicked cries and panting became louder as Isa neared the girl in trouble. Suddenly, a blur of pastel ran past the trees. Following her, Ayden screeched.

Isa nodded in understanding.

From within the trees, the girl's features were slender and soft, with long almost midnight black straight hair that perfectly complimented her rich dark brown skin. Gold jewelry encompassed her wrists, ankles, and hair which seemed to sparkle in the sun. Her arms and hands were covered in red cultural markings distinguishing her as Endrancian. She looked sophisticated and regal, but terrified and exhausted.

Suddenly, the girl tripped over a root scrambling to get up, but not before Isa caught up with her. She carefully approached the girl, with a dagger hidden behind her back.

"Are you from the capital?" Isa asked.

The girl looked maybe a year younger than Isa but Endrancian Royalty. Seeing her get closer and closer, she quickly picked up a rock holding it defensively.

"What do you want?" Her Endrancian accent came through her teeth.

"I'm not going to hurt you," Isa reassured her. The girl briefly glanced at Ayden who was perched on Isa's shoulder.

"Now, let's put the rock down," she said placing a hand over her heart. After a second of silence, the girl nodded slowly dropping the rock.

*"What's her name? Ask her,"* Ayden asked from Isa's shoulder.

"I don't know," Isa whispered back to him as he ruffled his feathers. The girl opened her mouth slightly.

"You-, you can talk to animals?" The girl pointed at Ayden. Isa didn't answer.

"What's your name?" She asked instead, trying to move closer to the royal.

"Amarantha Rafiq."

Isa nodded.

"Where do you come from?"

Amarantha paused deciding whether she could trust Isa.

"The capital. I'm escaping from an arranged marriage," Amarantha whispered shyly thinking the trees could hear her.

Turning to the falcon next to her, Isa said, "Ayden go to Deval, make sure no one followed her."

*"Right."*

Ayden flew off Isa's shoulders and back into the forest. Isa turned to Amarantha.

"An arranged marriage?"

Amarantha nodded.

"Well, I'm not going to turn you in if that's what you're worried about," Isa said grinning twirling her dagger back into its sheath. Amarantha eyed it curiously, before speaking.

"I need your help, please. I-,I can pay you," Amarantha said as she interlocked her hands as if about to beg.

*Should I?* Isa thought. *What if someone came looking for her?*

But before she could answer, Amarantha's eyes rolled back and she fainted in exhaustion.

Isa sighed.

<hr>

The stars hung overhead as the sparks from the fire casted a soft glow against the trees around them.

Amarantha shocked herself awake finding Isa roasting a rabbit over the fire she had made. Lifting the blanket that Isa had placed over her, Amarantha looked down to see her clothes had changed.

"Welcome back," Isa said, her rich brown hair braided over her shoulder. Amarantha found a water skin beside her, prying it open before gulping down the cool liquid.

"Thank you," she replied quietly watching her.

Isa nodded as she sat on a fallen log.

"It's not my business, but I'm wondering why an arranged marriage? To whom?" She asked leaning an arm on her knee, poking the fire.

"My father, King of Endrancia, recently agreed to a political and economic treaty agreement with your king to stop the years of violence between our countries. An arranged marriage was agreed to seal the alliance," Amarantha paused wrapping her arms around her legs.

Isa raised her dark eyebrows. Isa knew about the unrest and tension with Endrancia since she had played a part in it as a soldier.

"I was not able to convince my father otherwise. He is quite traditional you see, but what upset me the most was that they didn't think to ask me. One day, I was sparring with my brother, and the next thing I knew I was in a carriage over the border heading to marry your Prince.

I was barred from leaving the grounds of the citadel at Al-Kurma before I was whisked away here.

On the way to Deval, we were stopped on the road and attacked. Most of my guards died fighting the monsters off. They were not from Endrancia or Atalia. We had been getting reports of these creatures from our southern border near the Wastelands."

*Attacks from the Wastelands?* Isa furrowed her eyebrows.

The Princess continued.

"Once I made it to Deval, I was trapped again in another castle without any say. A few of my guards survived but I was scared for not only my safety but for my freedom. It was like living in a glass castle. Trapped, I could only see the world going on around me but I couldn't escape it." She looked up at Isa.

Clearing her throat, Isa pulled her brown eyes away from Amarantha's stare.

She looked down and continued poking at the fire as Amarantha spoke up again.

"I do not want anyone to find me," Amarantha pleaded as Isa watched her from the corner of her eye.

Seeing the face of the Princess looking at her as if this was her last chance. She made her decision.

Sighing and wiping her face, Isa nodded. Amarantha squealed in joy and came around to hug her before she could stop her. Isa's heart spiked about to push the Princess away but she stopped herself, accepting the hug.

The next morning, bright and early, Isa and Amarantha decided to use the main road and found passage with an older farmer who agreed to take them east to Queenside. The best place to hide Amarantha was with some old friends of Isa's.

They stopped at the local market to sell Amarantha's personal items. With Isa's clothes on Amarantha, no one questioned the two of them. If anything people were more interested in asking Isa about preparations for winter.

As the sky turned orange, the kind farmer dropped them off on the outskirts of Queenside. Thanking him and giving him some coin for their safe passage, Isa and Amarantha made their way into the small farming village.

Rolling green open fields covered the landscape as people's farms spread as far as the eye could see. Cows mooed watching them walk by.

"I'm going to take you to an old friend's farm," Isa told Amarantha as they walked alongside the stone walls.

Amarantha nodded.

"You will be safe with the Jones family until you decide when or where you want to go," Isa told her.

"This country is too cold for my liking, but if this is the taste of freedom then so be it," Amarantha commented, wrapping her arms around herself.

"Wait until the winter," Isa laughed as she stopped by a wooden gate opening it.

As they approached the property, firelight streamed from inside the glass windows of the stone house. They could hear the voices of laughter from the people inside.

Seeing Isa and Amarantha approach from the kitchen window, an older woman stepped out wiping her hands dry on her apron.

"Isa, I wasn't expecting you at this hour," she said as she walked closer to greet the girls. The woman didn't look a day over fifty but still had some grasp on youth.

"I came here to ask for a favor," Isa said turning towards Amarantha grasping her shoulders.

"This is Amarantha. She needs a place to stay for a while if you don't mind, Beth."

Beth looked at Amarantha noticing the Princess wouldn't look into her eyes.

"Mother? Who is it? Oh, hello Isa!"

Behind Beth, her only son, Quinn, stepped out from the door intrigued and immediately locked eyes with Amarantha.

"Come Amarantha, that's a beautiful name, why don't you come inside and have some food, you as well Isa," Beth added as she scooped Amarantha into her warm embrace and gestured her towards the door where Quinn introduced himself.

"I have to get back to Liliane as soon as possible," Isa said watching as Quinn's cheeks flushed red talking to Amarantha.

Beth frowned tsking.

"It is too dark to continue your journey. Come." Beth gestured her towards the door and ushered her inside. Isa chuckled at Beth's invitation already smelling the food from outside.

# CHAPTER 2

"Another one here, Bill." Isa waved her empty mug at the bartender and owner.

He nodded throwing a dish cloth over his burly shoulder.

"Sure thing, Isa!" He said filling up another client's cup.

Isa nodded and smiled.

Since her friend and roommate Victoria worked in The Lazy Cat Inn in the middle of the small village of Liliane. Isa enjoyed free drinks every once in a while. Besides, Ginger shared all of the tidbits about Bill and the Inn with her whenever the cat was awake.

The window shutters of the Inn were open, letting in the summer breeze from the forest as Isa reminisced on her hometown. Liliane was surrounded by thatched buildings with a beautiful drinking fountain in the center of the square. The Lazy Cat Inn was located across from the local green as people strolled across the cobblestone.

Waiting for her drink, Isa suddenly frowned looking down at her hands deep in thought.

*To have a bit of wealth wouldn't be all that bad. Be able to eat good hearty food until I was full, bathe every day, and not have to worry about finding my next meal.*

Thinking about the Princess she had helped, Amarantha had given up her title and everything she knew for her freedom. *Was being a Princess all that bad? Amarantha was running away from an arranged marriage, so maybe in her case, yes.*

Footsteps echoed across the wooden floor as Victoria came walking over to her table bringing Isa out of her thoughts and another refill of her drink. Leaning back forward, Isa smiled up at her friend in thanks.

"You're getting tan and summer is almost over."

Isa titled her head at her.

"Well, that's what happens when you're outside all day."

Victoria let out a hearty laugh.

"What's the plan for the rest of the day?" Victoria

asked.

"Go to the orphanage and then go back home. Take a bath," Isa shrugged.

Victoria scoffed waving her hand near her nose.

"You better."

Bill called Victoria back to work.

"Yeah, yeah, I'm coming!" Victoria yelled back standing up and smiling at Isa before going back behind the bar. Isa watched her friend before taking another drink from her mug, her shoulder relaxing.

Then, the bell chimed over the bar door as another newcomer walked into the pub. The men at the bar kept laughing and talking among themselves until a tenor voice bled through the chatter.

Turning to the side, Isa glanced at the black clothed figure not recognizing him from anywhere. He had soft wheat blond curls that framed his soft but defined face. Isa couldn't help but notice his slender but athletic build. A white wooden bow was slung across his back alongside a packsack. But he had no quiver or arrows.

He was attractive, she concluded as she continued to observe him.

Through the chatter, Isa heard him asking about the missing Princess of Endrancia. Isa kept looking at him from the corner of her eye. As Victoria cleaned a mug, she started pointing at Isa. Following her finger, he turned around and approached her table.

Isa waited until he was standing beside her.

"Excuse me, do you happen to know anything about the whereabouts of the missing Princess?"

Isa looked up at him, his blue eyes looking down at her.

"Why?" She shrugged as she sipped her drink.

Seeming to weigh his options, he sat down in the empty chair opposite her.

"Have you seen her? Do you possibly know anything that can help me find her?" He asked worried.

Isa was silent.

His eyes. It was his blue eyes that caught her off guard.

"What if I did?"

Taming his frustration surprisingly well, he rubbed the stubble on his chin with his hand as he started to look a bit flustered. Was *he* intimidated by her?

"Her family has paid me for her safe return back to the capital," he said almost at a whisper.

This was what Isa was afraid of, someone from the capital trying to find Amarantha.

"So you want to bring her back?"

"That's the plan, yes. Can you help me?" He asked giving a slight smile. She nodded agreeing to help him.

"Really? Why?" He asked leaning back as Bill came to them and placed a full drink in front of him.

"First of all, you seem concerned about her wellbeing or you wouldn't be asking me all these questions. If you were in it for the money, I would be wasting your time-."

"Isa!" Moore burst through the door of the Inn as everyone turned to look at her. Standing up quickly, Isa stepped around the table.

"Isa, where are you?" Moore asked before finding her.

"What's wrong, Moore?" She asked. Moore panted pointing outside.

"I need your help! I don't know what's happened to Tom! He just collapsed."

Moore's eyes were wide with distress as Isa nodded. Rushing out of the pub with Moore, they could see a crowd of people gathered around a body.

"Move!" Moore shouted as Isa immediately jumped to

Tom's body kneeling beside him.

"Tom, can you hear me, what's happened?"

Tears fell down his face as his body seized in pain.

"Isa, help me. It burns," he croaked out his hands shaking as his fingers turned a sickening black. Isa heard Moore's cries from behind her as she tried to find the cause.

It looked like poison but from what? This looked just like what happened to the others.

"I'm here, we are all here," she said calmly. The veins on Tom's arms were turning black as the poison traveled up his arm making him hiss in pain. Dark magic wafted off him as Isa blinked the tears away from her eyes.

"Tom, Tom, listen to me," Isa said knowing she couldn't heal him.

"Don't be afraid. You will find peace, let Death guide you." With her words, she placed a hand on his forehead as Tom let out a breath. Lifting a shaking hand, Tom reached out to Moore.

"I love you so much." His voice cracked as Moore nodded whispering the same to him.

His body stopped shaking as his hand went limp in

Moore's grasp. Sobbing, Moore placed her head on his stomach.

Isa stood watching Moore as the concerned eyes of the town's people looked at her.

"Isa?" Kate stepped forward.

"More people are dying. We are getting word from the other villages that hundreds of their people have passed, children too."

"We can't keep living like this, in fear!" Another person spoke up. They were silent until Kate turned back to Isa.

"You have to go and see the King," she said as the other people agreed with her. Isa's heart spiked, but she still nodded her head.

"I will plead to the King for his help," she stated.

"This is all your fault!"

Isa turned to see John with some other men pointing accusatory fingers at the newcomer who was speechless and in shock.

"He is not at fault here," Isa sighed but her words fell upon deaf ears.

Grasping his black shirt, John pushed him back into the stone wall of the pub.

"He's with me John so let him go."

"Is he now? We've heard you've been asking questions and now with Tom's death-," John said as the stranger surprisingly stood his ground with only his bow slung across his back.

*Nothing good would come out of this.* Walking up to them, she grabbed John's forearm making him turn towards her.

"Yes, he is," Isa reiterated standing in front of him. "So back off and go home to Abbie." She commanded.

"Alright, have your fun with him Isa, bring him back in one piece. We didn't mean no harm," John laughed as he left.

"People here don't like those who ask too many questions. Let's get going before it turns dark," Isa stated turning towards the stranger who smoothed down his shirt.

"Wait, you're going to take me to Amarantha?" He asked.

"Yes. I have my own priorities to settle first," she stated heading back into the pub. The stranger followed closely behind her.

"By the way, I'm Orion. Thank you for helping me."

As Isa led Orion through town, she immediately noticed that he was quite inquisitive.

"How are you not affected by all these deaths then?"

Isa stopped to look at him furrowing her eyebrows.

"Of course this is taking a toll on me. But I've seen too many deaths in my life."

He nodded.

"You have a lot of game in your bag. I see you like to hunt?" Orion asked as they walked side by side on the cobblestone road.

"But you don't have a bow on you?" He continued.

Isa stopped in her tracks again and turned towards him, getting a little annoyed.

"My staff here can shift into a bow, watch." She pulled her staff off the extra leather bindings on her back and with a light shake, it transformed into a bow and a quiver full of arrows appeared on her leg holster.

Orion seemed impressed.

"You know magic?"

"Only some basic magic. What about you? You carry a

bow but no arrows?" Isa asked as she shook her bow again to turn it back into a staff.

"I'm a light sorcerer."

Isa turned her head in surprise.

"A light sorcerer? I thought only the members of the royal family were capable of doing that type of magic?" She asked as Orion seemed to freeze completely.

"There are more of us out there. You know," he said forcing a smile.

They continued walking as Isa and Orion followed the path covered by an orchard of trees. Then they reached an iron gate that read *Ms. Whittle's Home for Orphan Children*.

"This is our first stop," Isa said to Orion.

"An orphanage?" He asked a little confused.

The orphanage had been Isa's only home ever since she could remember and thankfully, most of her memories had been good ones. Since then, Isa had always tried to help everyone at the orphanage as much as she could. Especially now with the bizarre deaths happening in the other villages.

The sound of familiar voices and screams of the children made Isa smile. As they walked closer to the ivy-covered stone manor, they heard Ms. Whittle's gentle voice telling the children that someone was at the door.

"Coming!"

Isa chuckled.

Ms. Whittle's wrinkled but kind face appeared from behind the wooden door. Her auburn greying hair was up in a bun and tied with a ribbon that one of the children made for her.

Seeing Isa, her face lit up.

"Oh dear, it is so good to see you! How did your latest hunt go?" Ms. Whittle asked as she pulled Isa into a bone-crushing hug. Isa felt at home again.

"Hi, Ms. Whittle. It was good thanks," Isa said pulling out of her embrace.

"I came to drop off some goodies." The children ran from behind the door and immediately noticed Orion strolling across the lawn.

"Children be careful!" Ms. Whittle called out to them but to no avail. As cheers and giggles filled the silence in front of them, Isa and Ms. Whittle watched as the children were talking all at once to Orion. One of the younger kids pointed at him while shouting at Isa and Ms. Whittle.

"Isa brought a boy home!" Isa immediately reeled back as Ms. Whittle laughed as the kids started chanting "*Isa has a suitor!*"

"Come here you little rascals!" Isa ran towards the group of children as they all screamed.

"He looks like a nice man. I would even say from the nobility, I just hope he is what you need," Ms. Whittle added crossing her arms watching her.

Isa sighed pretending to ignore her comment. Suddenly, she felt a tug on her leg and looked down to see little six-year-old Emily with her thumb in her mouth.

"What can I do for you, Emily?" Isa asked kneeling down to her height as the dark blonde-haired girl looked at her eagerly.

"Why do you carry all those weapons?" Startled by her question, Isa looked up at Ms. Whittle for permission before answering.

"Well, I carry all these weapons so I can protect you!" Isa grinned putting on a face and messing up Emily's hair making her giggle before standing back. Hearing screams from the other kids, Ms. Whittle finally interfered.

"Now children, it's time to come inside."

Some of them waved and said bye to Isa on their way back as she did the same. Once everyone was back inside, Isa finally dropped her pouch on the ground crouching down and opening it up.

"Take your pick." Isa spread the carcasses out to display them for Ms. Whittle, who dropped down to her level examining the carcasses.

"Who is he?" She asked nodding her head at Orion as she looked at Isa's game selection. Isa turned around to see him roaming around waving at the kids from the window.

"His name is Orion. He is coming with me to the capital. It's happened again, Ms. Whittle. Another unexplainable death. The people in town want me to go and plead for help to the King," Isa whispered turning back around to see Ms. Whittle with her eyebrow raised.

"Just be careful."

"I promise I will be. Please keep the children safe," Isa said trying to be reassuring.

Ms. Whittle finally chose a carcass as Orion stepped

closer.

"How much do I owe you?" Ms. Whittle asked, but Isa brushed her off.

"You don't owe me anything," Isa told Ms. Whittle as she smiled at her. Ms. Whittle placed one of her hands on Isa's shoulder and then on her cheek.

"You are too good for us, Isa."

"Safe travels, my dear," Ms. Whittle said as they finally said goodbye. With one last farewell cheek kiss, Ms. Whittle closed the manor door behind her as Isa walked back to where Orion was standing.

"Alright, first stop done, one more to go," Isa said rubbing her hands together, waiting to see Orion's reaction.

"One more?" He questioned happily not seeming upset. She nodded.

◆

Once Isa and Orion were back into the main square of Liliane, out of nowhere, they heard window shutters crashing and cries. Turning the corner, across the street, Isa panicked seeing that it was her window shutter that had splintered. Luckily, the old cobbler below them had gone home by now.

"Shit! What happened this time?" Isa suddenly broke out into a run. Orion looked at her confused but followed her.

"Wait, how often does this happen?" Orion questioned trying to keep up, sprinting up the stone steps.

"More than you think."

Isa burst through the door to find Victoria crying and throwing different belongings and clothes all over the place. Nervously, Laura followed behind a fuming Victoria trying to calm her friend down. But Victoria was in a rage and couldn't be stopped.

"That fucking shit, Damien! I walked in after work and found him sleeping with another woman!" Victoria yelled with her eyes red in fury as she continued throwing his things out of the broken window.

Assessing the damage and seeing that no one was injured, Isa placed her hand on her chest. Sighing, she inspected the window as she was thinking about how much a new window shutter was going to cost. Standing up straight again, Isa noticed Laura trying to comfort Victoria.

"Thank god you aren't hurt. What are we going to tell the landlord tomorrow?" Isa asked as they both turned noticing her presence. Victoria walked up to Isa and firmly grasped her shoulders.

"My heart is broken, Isa! And all you're thinking about is a broken window?" Victoria shook her as Laura came up behind Victoria to ease her off Isa's shoulders.

"He was your fifth partner this year?" Isa questioned as Laura gestured for her to stop talking from behind Victoria.

"True," Victoria paused not denying it.

"I mean do we choose men for their personality or for how good they are in bed hm?" Victoria asked herself raising her eyebrows as Isa covered her mouth in surprise trying to hide her laugh.

"Victoria!" Isa exclaimed, surprised at her comment.

"Now, now Victoria, mind your words, we have a guest in our home," Laura said calmly as they both finally took notice of Orion standing there awkwardly behind Isa.

Victoria perked up and her mood immediately changed.

"Oh, you're the one from the pub?" Raising her eyebrows looking at him up and down, Victoria hummed observing him.

"What's your name?" Victoria asked putting a hand on her hip watching him. Orion stepped out from behind Isa.

"I'm Orion," he said half waving half smiling.

"Isa never brings anybody home let alone members of the opposite sex," Laura said reaching around Isa to shake Orion's hand.

"I'll leave some meat behind for you on the table, Laura," Isa said heading into her room.

"Wait, hold on. Isa, you are not leaving yet. I'm preparing dinner tonight," Laura remarked towards Isa.

"We'll stay. But on the condition that you go easy on him, Victoria," Isa called from the hallway to her room.

"I make no promises, Isa," Victoria said raising a singular eyebrow.

Orion gulped.

# CHAPTER 3

The sky had turned a blissful red and orange, but it was starting to get chilly in the evenings. Isa could tell that the autumn season was coming which would lead to yet another hard winter.

As Isa finished clearing some dirt and making a circle of rocks for the fire, Orion placed the pile of sticks and wood beside her. Wiping his hands in triumph, he went back to his own packsack to pull out his sleeping mat.

Orion hadn't said a word to her since leaving Isa's tenement. But he seemed cheerful enough, so maybe Victoria didn't scare him off. His silence didn't bother her. As Isa threw another log onto the increasing fire, she wondered where Ayden was.

Orion walked up to her and sat on the log rubbing his hands together over the fire making Isa look up at him curiously.

"I haven't had that much fun in years."

Isa let out a hearty laugh as she raised her eyebrows in disbelief at his comment.

"You think so? Victoria didn't scare you?" She chuckled as she poked the fire moving the glowing red ashes around.

"She was surprisingly nice. Where did you meet them?" Orion asked curiously as Isa laughed at him.

"The three of us grew up in the orphanage. Ms. Whittle told us that Victoria's parents were pirates that died off the coast of Atalia since she was found with a pirate amulet around her neck. It's like her good luck charm. Less is known about Laura's parents. Once we were old enough, Laura and Victoria moved in together in Liliane and I joined them a couple of years later," Isa paused sighing. "They have always been there for me through thick and thin."

Ms. Whittle told Isa very little about her past except that her mother had died giving birth to her and that she knew nothing about Isa's father.

"You are different. You seem to carry a lot on your shoulders. I can tell the people from Liliane respect you,"

Orion said softly.

"I feel different. Constantly surviving, living, and trying to stay alive. I want to have a quiet, peaceful and happy life. I'm trying to find some normality and healing in my life. The world is cruel," Isa ended looking down and poking the fire again.

"Does this have anything to do with what little Emily had asked you earlier?" Not expecting that, Isa lifted her head to look at Orion. She nodded.

"Sort of. Not only do I carry these weapons to protect others but also to protect myself. It's not safe for a young woman traveling alone these days," Isa continued.

"You never know where you might end up one day or the next. I've had to deal with people taking advantage of others. On top of that, to deal with all the men who think they are privileged," Isa added lifting a hand. Orion nodded his head in understanding.

Isa lifted herself off the log and finally laid out her sleeping mat. Rummaging through her pack, she brought out her small map of Atalia as well as her compass.

She wanted to make sure that they were following the footpath she had drawn through the forest.

Isa looked up as she turned to check on Orion. She found him laying down and reading a book using the fire as a light. Tilting her head, she questioned him.

"You bought a book with you?" Orion glanced to the side, nodding and smiling at her.

*This just confirmed that Orion was probably born into some kind of wealth or nobility. Amarantha's parents had probably hired him because they knew him. But what about the Prince? Why hadn't he come to find her?* She thought chuckling to herself.

"You alright?" Coming out of her trance, Isa turned to Orion who had put his book down worried about her.

"I'm fine," Isa grinned as she finished preparing for bedtime. "Anyway, it's going to be a long day of traveling tomorrow so get some rest."

Stepping back onto her sleeping mat, Isa found the wool blanket Ms. Whittle had made her and used it to wrap around herself

Closing her eyes and calming her breath, Isa felt the last bit of heat coming from the put out fire. As she was trying to fall asleep, she kept one ear on Orion. Still not fully trusting him, she hid a small dagger underneath her head as she heard Orion rustle about.

She expected complete silence after that.

"Goodnight, Isa."

Opening her eyes in surprise, Isa didn't know how to respond to Orion. No one had said goodnight to her since she was back in the orphanage.

Isa swallowed.

"Night."

<hr>

The next day, they packed up their camp and started their journey through the forest. The morning dew stuck to the leaves and the dirt, their footprints making imprints on the forest floor beneath them. Orion was silent.

But Isa had a plan.

In and out quick, simple, and quietly. She'd find her way to the castle and demand an audience with the King.

"You know it's interesting that there are so many plants that heal but also can kill you, you know? If you don't know which one to eat or pick, you could die," Orion blabbed as she stepped over a branch.

"Mhm." Isa hummed rubbing her eyes.

"I remember reading once about this plant called Deaths Winterberry also known as *Mortem Idaeus*," Orion stated as Isa perked up stopping to turn around and look at him curiously.

"Ooo, look at you knowing your rare plants. Who did you learn that from?" She asked teasing him.

"My mother, she-," Orion continued but Isa shushed him. He looked up at her worried.

"What?" Orion asked but Isa didn't say anything scanning the forest around them.

She had heard voices and the distress calls of an animal. Turning to the right, Isa picked up her pace as she jumped over fallen tree trunks leaving Orion behind with a confused face. The voices grew louder as Isa could make out the sounds of a struggle. Finally coming up to the clearing, Isa crouched and hid behind a bush, watching and waiting.

In the clearing, there were men in grey and brown leather clothing trying to corral a white unicorn with spears. The creature was rearing and snorting trying to use its horn defensively. Isa noticed the red blood stains on the pure white coat of the animal and she narrowed her eyes knowing what they were doing.

Hearing rustling behind her, Orion popped out from the trees. Trying to make him go quiet, Isa pushed him down next to her roughly by his shoulders so they wouldn't be seen.

"What's going on?" Orion asked as he regained himself seeing the men trying to spear the unicorn into a cage near their carriage.

"Poachers, I assume," Isa whispered surveying the scene as she removed her bow from around her back. Nocking an arrow, she observed.

"But that's illegal," Orion added turning towards her in shock. Isa shrugged.

"That doesn't stop them."

Unicorns were some of the purest beings and Atalia's national animal. Their horns held great magical properties and was worth a lot of money. They both watched as the unicorn was finally captured and pushed into the cage.

"We have to help it," Orion said as his shoulder shook. Isa turned towards him furrowing her eyebrows.

"No, let me-, you can't just jump-."

Before she could finish, Orion jumped up out of the bushes and towards the group. Isa tried to grab him but it was too late. Still crouching behind the bushes, she watched as Orion blindly ran into the clearing. *What did he think he was doing?*

"Well shit," she whispered seeing the scene unfold before her eyes. Orion only had his bow with him so what would that do? Slapping a hand on her forehead, Isa shook her head as Orion approached the poachers.

"Let the creature go, I command you!" He shouted as the group turned towards him.

They smirked and started laughing at him as Orion kept demanding to release the unicorn. Pointing their spears at him, Orion knew he had been rash as his eyes widened.

"Come on, can't we talk about this? Just let the unicorn go," he said holding his hands up in surrender.

"Great," Isa said underneath her breath rolling her eyes.

Running towards the group, she stepped out from behind Orion and twirled her staff around hitting every single man that tried to approach her.

As he watched, Orion couldn't help but notice how smoothly and easily Isa started fighting with her staff. It was like a dance, her steps precise and making sure she didn't exert too much energy. Her staff was like an extension of her arm as they made their mark.

He had only seen that type of fighting in Deval.

Orion pulled the cage door open and the unicorn stepped out but didn't leave. Orion looked at it worried and confused, but then he heard the last body drop to the ground and followed the unicorn's line of sight.

Isa was barely even breathing hard as she scoffed at all the unconscious bodies.

Taking a deep breath before slinging the staff back across her back, Isa stepped towards the unicorn who was watching her intently. Isa knelt down with an arm on her knee. Seeing this, the unicorn moved its front leg underneath its body lowering its head to the ground in a bow.

The unicorn was giving her a salute. This was such an extremely rare sight. To get the respect and thanks of a unicorn was one of the highest magical blessings someone could receive. A unicorn was able to read one's soul.

*"Thank you for your service."* The unicorn rose back onto its hooved feet.

"You're welcome. Thank you," she said to the unicorn as she stood up. The creature approached her nudging its muzzle to her chest as Isa smiled accepting it and rubbed its face. The unicorn turned towards Orion. Standing still, he watched the unicorn before bowing giving its blessing towards him as well.

"*He is a good man.*" The unicorn told Isa before disappearing into the forest.

As Orion's heartbeat pounded in his ears, he realized something. The unicorn must have known who he was.

"What did the unicorn say to you?" He asked coming up to her intrigued

"Come Orion, we need to keep moving," Isa said while walking back into the forest.

Hearing the groans of one of the poachers, Orion looked down before kicking him back into unconsciousness. Orion chuckled to himself crossing his arms. Then, he jogged to catch up with Isa.

"You can talk to animals? How long have you been able to do that?"

Isa sighed giving a slight nod of her head.

"Ever since I was little, I've always been able to talk to

animals. It's like a mind magic, I can only understand animals that have the capacity to communicate with humans themselves."

Orion was silent.

"Does that make sense?"

"Not really." Orion smiled at her.

That night when they made camp and had some dinner, Isa turned to Orion who was poking at the fire.

"You shouldn't have done that," she stated.

"I had to. What were they going to do with the creature?" Orion asked. She sighed turning serious.

"Unicorns are sold as pets to wealthy lords and their magic horns are used as medicine for the underground market. To be honest, you didn't need to rush in like that."

Orion looked down at the ground.

"It was the right thing to do."

Isa turned to Orion seeing him in a new light, especially after what the unicorn had said. Isa knew there was more to Orion than what he was telling her. That night, she didn't hide her dagger underneath her head.

⸻ ⬦ ⸻

Orion woke up to the birds chirping in the trees above him.

Sitting up and stretching, Orion chuckled to himself before he realized that Isa's sleeping mat was empty. Confused, he looked around until he heard Isa's voice from the edge of the trees.

He knew she wouldn't have gone far.

He walked past the tree line and found Isa crouched down next to the side of the small cliff overlooking the main paved gravel road. She had her staff in her hand for balance and a falcon perched on her shoulder. Isa laughed at something as the falcon ruffled their feathers.

"Morning."

Isa turned over her shoulder to acknowledge him.

"Well, good morning to you too sleepy head," she chuckled grinning at him as Orion reached up to smooth down his hair.

"Orion this is Ayden, Ayden this is Orion." Orion nodded at the falcon as Isa turned back to face the road.

"Why are you watching the road?"

"Ayden here says that there's a carriage coming."

Orion raised his eyebrows not knowing what to say.

Isa stood up as Ayden flew off her shoulder. Turning to Orion, she shook her staff into a bow and her quiver appeared.

"Can you keep a secret?" Isa said as she turned to look directly at Orion.

"Yes, of course, why?" Orion asked curiously but that's all she needed to know.

As the carriage lined up right below them, Isa nocked an arrow and immediately released it sending the arrow to land right in front of the horses. Startled, the animals reared making the carriage driver halt. Stunned, Orion's eyes widened. The horse neighed in fright as Isa jumped swiftly from the cliff and to the top of the carriage.

Opening the carriage door, she made the lord fall out roughly out of his carriage and onto the stone paved road. Once he was spluttered on the ground, Isa swiftly jumped into the wheeled carriage rummaging through it.

Orion was shocked.

Isa chuckled as she found what she was looking for. Holding up the bag of gold coins, Isa whistled to Ayden. Once he was close, she threw the bag above her head as the falcon grabbed it.

Scared, the lord looked up at her and finally noticed that she was a girl.

"How dare you!" He exclaimed, offended. "How dare you, a woman of your ungodly stature, do this sort of thing to me?"

"You should be hanged, you whore!"

"Go back to the fires of hell where you belong!"

"Ungodly stature? Hell?" Isa stated as she reached out to him, pulling him by the scruff of his collar.

"Is that all you could come up with?" Isa rolled her eyes. Letting him go, she walked back to search the rest of the carriage one last time.

Orion was stunned.

He was learning more and more about Isa and the people of Atalia as the days progressed. How much was she keeping from him?

Everyone had secrets.

Climbing back up the cliff, Isa walked past Orion, picking up the bag of gold and gestured for him to follow her back into the trees toward their camp.

*Who was this person? She saved him and the unicorn from the poachers with just a swing of her weapons. But she also looted the lord who stole from her people. Who was this girl?* He thought.

Taking a deep breath, Orion hoped that she would still take him to Amarantha, but he was not sure anymore.

Suddenly, his head felt dizzy as his vision blurred.

Orion fainted.

# CHAPTER 4

Groaning awake, Orion placed a hand over his forehead. Lifting himself up, he placed his hands over his eyes. The incident with the lord had shaken him up as he couldn't stop thinking about everything that had happened.

From the top of Isa's shoulder, Ayden nudged her head with his wing. Noticing Orion had woken up, Isa sighed pulling the already sorted bag of gold from her belt.

"Welcome back," she said tossing half of it to Orion.

"What's this?" He asked quietly looking at both her and the falcon.

"It's payment for keeping your mouth shut. And I don't know how much Amarantha's family paid you, but this is so you don't have to take her back." Orion nodded and placed it into his pack before noticing the other red velvet bag of gold that Isa was putting more gold into.

"What are you going to do with your share of the money and that other bag?" Orion asked as Isa packed up their camp.

"Use it to gain an audience with the King," she said holding up the red velvet bag, "this is for Liliane and for the family that has Amarantha."

"With a family? She is safe in Atalia, then?" Orion asked excitedly. Isa quickly looked up from her feet realizing her mistake.

"Shit." Isa cringed under her breath.

"*Shit indeed.*" Ayden ruffled his feathers.

Isa smacked her forehead.

Dumb, stupid, idiot. She had let her guard down.

Isa sighed, not saying anything, trekking back into the forest with Orion behind her.

After a while of walking, Isa found a fallen tree trunk to rest on for a little bit as Ayden flew off her shoulder and onto the ground in front of her. Dropping her pack on the ground with a humph, she stretched her back out as she waited for Orion to follow. She watched him as he sat down next to her.

Bending down to reach into her pack, Isa pulled out

her water skin, some bread wrapped in wax paper, and a dead mouse from a side pocket. Tossing the dead mouse for Ayden, she opened the wax paper and handed some bread to Orion. Isa took her half and sighed looking down at her piece of bread before taking a bite.

"Look, I don't need to explain my actions to anyone," Isa said but he didn't say anything. Orion side glanced at her before looking back down at the bread.

"First of all, that lord deserved it," Isa paused using her thumb to point behind her.

"Please continue," Orion said in between bites. He was still waiting for her explanation. Isa faced forward not ready to look at him.

"When I signed up for the war, the benefits for the royal army were great, especially for the orphanage. I was placed in the cavalry since I could talk to animals which seemed like the best option for me. In a short time, I climbed up in the ranks," Isa paused, remembering.

"I was accepted into the special forces right when I turned eighteen. After about a year of intense training, I was deployed outside of Atalia. I come back home and was released due to injuries." At this, Orion turned to her but didn't say anything.

Isa remembered those gruesome and intense training moments that she had to endure just to be taken seriously.

"I've gotten a bit rusty over the years, but I still got it," Isa chuckled softly nudging Orion's shoulder trying to make him laugh a little, which worked.

"Don't you need to have combat experience to even apply for the special forces let alone get accepted? You can't just get in straight from basic training."

Isa slowly smiled as Orion finally looked up to question her. Seemed like he was feeling better. Picking up her stuff as she swung her pack onto her back readjusting the straps, Isa answered.

"I'll tell you while we keep walking," Isa said as Orion seemed to perk up. Having finished as well, Ayden jumped up and flew back onto Isa's shoulder.

"Yes, I was accepted into the special forces not even a year of being in the royal army, but that was because a retired knight trained me," she said as Orion finally came up to walk beside her.

"A retired knight?" He asked curiously.

"Yes. He passed through Liliane many years ago when I

was younger, and I begged him to teach me how to fight. I guess he saw something in me since he taught me pretty much everything he knew from fighting to just basic everyday survival. I probably wouldn't be here without his guidance. He inspired me to join the army."

Isa smiled remembering her old mentor.

"What was his name if you don't mind me asking?"

Isa turned to Orion shaking her head.

"Not at all, his name was Sir Alexander. He gifted Ayden to me after he left," Isa said pointing to her falcon friend, and as on cue, Ayden kacked at him.

"Wait, I knew him." Orion turned to her sharply.

"You knew him?" She raised an eyebrow.

"Uh yes, I did," he coughed as Isa followed next to him. "Well, I've heard his stories."

———◆———

As the sky grew dark and cloudy, Isa and Orion finally reached the little hamlet town of Crasmere. It was a small lumber village and the wooden buildings were built around and into the trees. The houses almost seemed to have sprouted from the branches fauna around them.

The lanterns lit up the gravel and dirt roads enough for her to make her way to her favorite spot, the Black Sow Inn. Walking through the door, the little bell chimed. In the middle of the bar was the trunk of a tree as the inn and bar seemed to be built around it. Branches of leaves covered the ceiling as Marguerite, the Innkeeper and owner, acknowledged them.

"Isa! Welcome, welcome!" She said gesturing them inside. Marguerite was curvy and plumb with cheer, happiness, and warmth.

Rounding the corner of her bar, she scooped Isa into a hug. From behind them, Orion stood looking around the tavern in awe of the architecture as Isa smiled at her friend.

"Please Marguerite, some dinner and two rooms for me and my friend," Isa said as Marguerite released her nodding enthusiastically.

"Of course, of course, anything for you, Isa. Now sit down both of you!" Marguerite waved them off to a table in the corner of the pub next to the roaring fireplace where a boar was being roasted filling the room with homey aromas.

As they sat down at the empty round table, Orion turned to Isa.

"How do you know Marguerite?" He asked slinging his bow across the arm of the chair.

"I helped put the Inn on the map. I found this place when I originally started in the cavalry and ever since then I've spread the word and brought patrons for Marguerite to take care of. I was one of the first investors. Once the business was going well, I sold my portion to Marguerite so she would be the sole owner," Isa explained slinging an arm over the top of the chair to see if there was anyone she knew in the bar.

"That's-, that's so kind of you to do," Orion whispered watching her amazed. Isa shrugged as she leaned more into the fire trying to grasp as much warmth as she could.

Marguerite walked towards them.

"Isa is too humble. She sold her medal of honor from the King himself to help me start this Inn," Marguerite added placing two drinks in front of them. Orion's eyes widened.

"Your usual, Isa," she said brushing her hands across her apron.

Picking up the glass cup, Isa grinned wide and looked up at Marguerite.

"From your reserves?"

Marguerite waved her off smiling.

"Of course, some of Atalia's finest hydromel. On the house."

"Thank you."

"Supper should be right out soon," she stated smiling at them before turning back to the other patrons in the bar.

Once she was gone, Isa scooped the glass mug to her mouth letting out a breath of relief, the liquor calming her muscles. Turning back around to face Orion, Isa relaxed. As she drank, she placed her elbows on the table to rest her head in her palms.

"You received a medal of honor?" Orion asked. Isa sighed.

"I did. From my time in the special forces from the mission in Endrancia. Now you keep asking about me, but I don't know anything about you."

Orion seemed to hesitate a bit unsure before answering.

"Well, what do you want to know?" He said scratching the back of his head waiting for Isa's questions.

"Where were you born for starters?" She asked curiously.

"I was born in Deval on June 20th, in the year of our King 201. Six o'clock in the morning to be exact," Orion joked as Isa chuckled shaking her head. So Orion was just a couple of years older than herself, and Isa was right, he was from the capital.

"I see," Isa nodded, but Orion kept going.

"I grew up in Deval. I know that city like the back of my hand. Sadly, I grew up within the confines of the capital, so I haven't had much experience traveling outside of those stone walls. Deval has been the only place I have called home. I've only traveled once outside of Atalia, and it's made me want to travel even more." Orion paused as if wanting to say more before he looked at the fireplace as it cracked from behind Isa.

"Well, why don't you?" She asked, but he shook his head hesitating a bit before answering.

"I have duties back at home," Orion whispered as Isa nodded in understanding.

Before Isa could ask her next question, Marguerite came with two steaming plates of cooked pork and steamed vegetables. Saying their thanks and picking up the utensils from beside them, they both dug into their food. Then Isa swallowed pointing her fork at Orion as he chewed.

"What do you do then?" Isa asked changing the topic taking another bite from her pork. Orion shrugged cutting his vegetables.

"I mostly read and train with my father to be honest. Nothing too exciting." Orion swallowed chuckling watching Isa's deadpanned face from his comment.

"I didn't mean like everyday tasks, what do you do for work?" Isa rolled her eyes at Orion's response as she sliced another piece of pork.

"You could say I'm sort of an advisor in the castle."

Isa perked up at this, interested.

"Really? An advisor"

"Well sort of, I'm not-," Orion started.

"That's why Amarantha's parents paid you to bring her back?" Isa interrupted as she whispered thinking.

"Yes, I spent some time with her in the castle when she first came and she's nice, but-," Orion said but ended before he could complete his thought.

"Wait, this means you can get me an audience with the King?" Isa asked pointing a fork at him.

"Of course," Orion answered as Isa grinned before going back to her meal.

The fire was nice and warm as they enjoyed the comforts of having a roof over their heads and a warm hearth. A slurred drunken voice called out from behind the bar.

"Have any of you heard anything about the royal family lately?" A drunk patron turned around and addressed everyone in the tavern interrupting their conversation.

Furrowing her eyebrows, Isa turned her head intrigued and started watching the man get up and wobble about as others shook their heads.

"I've heard the prince is a wee sickly boy that never comes out of Deval!" Someone laughed as others started joining in with their drunken jokes clanging their mugs against each other's. Seeing them fall down in laughter, Isa turned to Orion who was watching them intensely.

"You look upset," Isa said pulling him from his thoughts.

"I'm alright." She didn't believe him.

"Then why -, oh you know the Prince, don't you?" Isa

said as he nodded.

"It's true that he's never ventured out of the capital. He really wants to learn about everything he can to be a good King as his father is," he whispered. She nodded respecting his answer.

She had met the King before when she received the medal of honor, but never the Prince. As Isa watched him, she could see the truth behind his blue eyes.

"I guess it's time to go to bed now. Marguerite?" Isa called as the innkeeper looked up from cleaning mugs.

"Yes, dear?" She asked.

"Which rooms are ours?" Isa asked standing up ready to head to bed.

"Up the hall and first one on the right for you, Isa. I've put your friend down the hall by the stables." Isa laughed as Orion grimaced a little.

"Finally, a real bed," she smiled as she got up collecting her things.

As he passed the bar where Marguerite was, Orion leaned in closer to her.

"The pork was lovely," Orion complimented with a smile. Marguerite smiled placing a hand over her heart.

"Oh thank you, dear. I hope the room is to your liking. Let me know if you need anything."

Orion nodded following behind Isa as they climbed the stairs. Coming up to the first room on the right, Isa opened the door to a straw mattress bed and a warm fire.

"Finally a real bed," Isa said before turning towards Orion.

"Have fun being woken up at dawn by the rooster," Isa teased watching Orion as he craned his neck to check which door was his.

"Night, Orion."

He grinned at her.

"Night, Isa."

# CHAPTER 5

Marguerite had insisted on a proper hearty breakfast before letting them continue on their journey into the forest.

As Orion came downstairs holding his lower back pulling loose pieces of straw from his hair, he joined Isa for breakfast. Eating his fill, he noticed that Isa used some of the coins that she had stolen from the lord to pay Marguerite, who was grateful for the money.

After they said their goodbyes to Marguerite, Isa noticed the grey clouds forming across the sky.

By the time it started to pour with rain, Isa and Orion were already trekking through the lush forest. Isa knew that it would be around the afternoon that they would reach the outskirts of Deval, so she would have to lead Orion through the path less walked to get there.

Her plan was to take him near the walls that surrounded

the city before confessing that she was never going to take him to where Amarantha was.

*Would he tell the King or even Amarantha's family what had happened?* She thought as they walked. *Would he get her an audience with the King?*

She had her doubts.

Letting out a soft curse, Orion almost tripped on the wet dark mud for the third time. Isa stopped to turn behind her making a face.

"Ok, ok, I get it," Orion replied.

"*Please be careful,*" Ayden kacked ruffling his wings shaking away the rain on top of Orion's shoulder.

Ayden had stayed perched on Orion's shoulder ever since that morning. Even though Orion couldn't understand him, he still seemed to enjoy Ayden's company.

A gnawing feeling clawed through Isa's stomach as they approached the outskirts of the city walls.

Dreading having to confront Orion she sighed closing her eyes. Opening them again, she turned around towards him as Ayden opened his beak but it was too late.

A hand grabbed her shoulder.

Immediately, Isa twisted the hand off her bending

down, sweeping her leg back as the black-clothed figure toppled over her and into the mud. But then more hands grabbed her pushing her knees to the ground.

Damnit.

Orion looked confused at the guards and the figure that had captured Isa, but she knew exactly who they were. Ayden screeched in panic flapping his wings on Orion's shoulder as he flew away from the scene. He already knew who they were and he had promised Isa he would flee if this ever happened.

Suddenly, General Adrastus stepped out from behind the trees looking straight at Isa, who didn't say anything or try to resist. Seeing the General, Orion stepped out in front of him sharply.

"What are you doing? Release her!" He commanded horrified at what was happening. But the General ignored Orion stepping around him like he wasn't even there.

Evening out her breathing, Isa stared at her former commander as he walked closer to her. Stopping in front of her, the guards at Isa's sides roughly made her stand up.

"General," Isa gritted out. The General of the special forces looked a lot older than the last time she had seen him. His bald head accentuated the rough but firm wrinkles on his face. Despite his age, he still looked like he could kill someone with his bare hands.

Orion stayed silent.

Isa glanced at him apologetically before turning back to stare at General Adrastus.

"Tsk, tsk Phantom, you of all people should have known this would happen if you ever tried to step foot inside the capital again. Did you believe I wouldn't have soldiers across Atalia keeping an eye on you?" General Adrastus wiggled his finger in front of Isa's face.

Suddenly, turning back around he swung an arm and punched Isa hitting her jaw. Coughing and hanging her head down in pain, Isa spat out some blood before looking up again.

The General continued.

"I thought that medal of honor would have kept you from coming back here ever again. I warned you this would happen if you ever tried to step foot into Deval again, so why come back?"

"My people-," she breathed out. "-are dying. I've come to ask to see the King."

General Adrastus stepped closer leaning down to whisper into her ear. Isa didn't flinch.

"The only reason I haven't done worse to you right now is because the Prince is watching."

Isa's eyes widened.

"Prince?" Isa whispered looking at Orion who was staring at Isa apologetically. He opened his mouth about to explain but he was interrupted.

"Oh, didn't you know? How exciting!" Isa's former General clapped his hands in glee, obviously enjoying seeing her suffer.

"My dear, this is Orion Dawn, the Prince of Atalia."

The Prince that Amarantha was running away from was Orion, the person she had just been traveling with these past couple of days. The person she had led back to the orphanage and her home.

*The crowned Prince of Atalia.* She couldn't believe it.

"Yes, you weren't the only one lying to one another," he said before he was interrupted by another guard who had gone through Isa's pack on her back.

"Sir, we found this in her possession," his voice called out as he held up Isa's half of the stolen coins.

"Stealing gold now, are we? Did I not train you to be better than having to steal from random nobles? Did time away from the force make you rusty, and for that matter, what's with all these mistakes? You're a disgrace!" General Adrastus laughed sarcastically at her.

"I choose you from the cavalry and this is how you turn out?"

Having paced in front of her, the General turned back around and punched her again on her nose. Grasping out in more pain, her legs shook. She used to be able to deal with great pain, but she had had a year's worth of rest and peace. She cursed her weak body.

"General, there is no need for this cruelty! Unhand her immediately!" Orion stated trying to calm the situation.

"Maybe some time in prison will do you some good, not like its anything new to you anyway. Take her away." With a flick of his wrist, Isa was pulled away bleeding from her nose and mouth.

"No! Let her go!" Orion shouted immediately trying to reach Isa, but another guard held him back. Helpless, he could only watch her being taken away. *Why wasn't she resisting? Fighting? Screaming? Anything? Isa had just let him hurt her, almost like she thought she deserved it.*

"She purposely deceived you, your majesty. She cannot be trusted," General Adrastus remarked not even glancing at Orion.

All Orion could think of that moment was Isa protecting Amarantha and risking her life for her people by coming back to the capital.

As the guards led her away, Isa turned to see Orion struggling against the guard holding him, but she shook her head looking back down at her feet.

———❧———

Orion pushed open the throne room doors as he marched straight to where his father was seated.

"Why did they take her? Release her immediately!" Orion demanded walking through the throne room.

Large white columns surrounded them with Atalian flags as his father's court members looked appalled by Orion's harsh behavior. The King dispersed his council with a wave of his hand as Orion stopped in front of him.

Looking down at his son, the King answered.

"My son, as I understand from General Adrastus, she

aided in the disappearance of Princess Amarantha and stole from Lord Byran, which is an act against Atalia," the King said sitting on the beautiful marble throne that had the faces of past Kings carved on it.

The King tried to calm his son down, but Orion wasn't having it.

"She must have had a good reason to help her," Orion pleaded trying to persuade his father.

"Despite that, we found marks done by barbarians on her back, scars from wartime-." Orion's eyes widened and he took in a sharp breath as he interrupted his father.

"You stripped her? How could you!"

"She is a criminal, Orion. With scars like that, she could be a spy. We still haven't completed negotiations with Endrancia yet. And she hid the Princess, so now we do not know where she is. How does that look for Atalia?" The King paused before continuing.

"And for that matter, why do you even value her life so much?"

"She protected Amarantha!"

"She interfered with a political treaty with Endrancia!" The King finally stood up in anger trying to end the conversation. They stared at each other until the King sighed realizing his outburst as he sat back down with a humph on his throne.

"You must understand that we need the Princess back for the arranged marriage, Orion. Don't you want peace and prosperity for your future Kingdom?" The King looked at his son tiredly.

"Yes father, but there must be another way. Neither of us wanted this marriage to begin with."

"I know you weren't happy with the agreement, but you have to realize that this is what's best for Atalia right now." Orion ignored his father's words as he thought.

Orion didn't want to leave Isa in the dungeons forever, he needed to convince his father to let her out and that she was innocent. Orion remembered something important that would probably get to his father.

"Have you already forgotten, father?" Orion looked up calmly watching to see his father's reaction.

"Forgotten what son?" The King asked while he held his head in annoyance and impatience.

"She was in the special forces," Orion said staring at his father.

"She?" He asked softly in confusion as he lifted his head and looked down at his son. *The soldier that escaped from Endrancia. Could it be?* The King thought. Gaining some confidence, Orion stood up fully and faced his father.

"You gave her a medal of honor, land, and wealth about a year ago," Orion paused hoping that his comment would sink in. "She is no criminal, but a solider. A war hero. She is more than that." He watched the gears work in his father's head.

"And since you won't, I'm going down there to apologize and explain everything to her."

"Wait, son-!"

Orion was gone before the King could say anything else. Sighing as he slumped against the throne and holding his head again, the King tried to control his emotions.

"You cannot stop him, my love."

The King looked up at his wife the Queen, who had stepped out from behind their thrones.

"Please my dear you did not need to hear that," Orion's father whispered finally relaxing a little bit after seeing his wife who had decided to stand right in front of him taking the hand on his face away from him.

"William, he is not a boy anymore," she said gently as she smoothed some of his dark greying hair away from his face.

"But he must understand, Alice; he will be King one day." He sighed as the Queen grinned at him, moving some of her braided dark blonde hair away from her face.

"I know that but remember when you were his age." She moved to hold his face in her hands making him look at her.

"Yes, and I met the most wonderful being in all the world and I fell in love with her. When she agreed to be my Queen, I was the happiest man alive," he said clasping over his wife's hands.

"Remember that feeling my dear. I can see the same spark in his eyes as yours when you were younger," she paused as the King nodded. "In addition, I'd like to meet this girl whom Orion is so eager to rescue from the dungeons."

# CHAPTER 6

Orion passed the guards who were surprised to see him, standing up abruptly and saluting him. But he headed straight to the keeper of keys and warden. Without even saying a word, the keeper of the keys opened the main entrance of the dungeons for him to walk into.

The warden led Orion through the stone maze of iron jails and finally came up to Isa's cell. He stood in front of her prison cell noticing her curled up against the rough stone wall. Her head leaned against the mossy stone as she watched through the small thin opening sitting on top of the rock slab that was supposed to be a bed.

Isa didn't acknowledge his presence.

She remained emotionless as a shiver ran through her body. The bruises already forming on her face, the dried blood caking her nose.

"I would like to be left alone, please," Orion said sternly.

"Of course, your majesty." The warden bowed and then left him alone. Orion grabbed the iron bars in front of him trying to get as close to Isa as possible.

"Isa, listen to me, please. It was not my intention for things to end up like this," Orion whispered to her hoping Isa was listening to him.

A drop of water splashed between them.

"I'm sorry, Isa," Orion whispered as he opened his eyes again to see that Isa hadn't moved at all.

"I'll get you out of there as soon as I can."

---

Isa watched the people down below as the sky turned dark speckled with lanterns. The citizens of the capital all looked so happy going about their day.

Orion had left a while ago looking so helpless and her chest ached in guilt. Sighing, she felt bad having ignored Orion like that, but she needed to get her point across. *How could he have not told her he was the Prince?*

Isa's priority at that moment was to get out of her

prison cell. Having been in and around the castle prisons more than she would have liked, she knew the mechanisms of the locks.

Waiting as a guard walked past her cell telling the prisoners to sleep for the night, Isa watched him go. Having tracked the guard rotations for the day, she made her move to escape when they were on their break.

Reaching down, Isa zipped down the secret pocket in her boots and pulled out her lock-picking system. Sitting up from the slap of concrete and being mindful of the rats on the floor, she stepped over them and towards the door.

Kneeling by the door, Isa blindly reached around to the cell lock.

Grabbing it, she placed the unlocked lock on the ground smirking to herself. Isa stood up as she carefully pushed open the cell door and gently closed it again not to disturb the other prisoners. Like a shadow underneath the cover of darkness, Isa snuck her way through the stone hallways of the prison.

"Achoo!" Isa quickly covered her mouth. Her sneeze echoed across the stone room as she held her breath waiting for the guards to catch her. One of the armored guards looked around before turning to his partner beside him nudging his steel shoulder.

"Did you sneeze?"

Offended, his partner slowly turned his head.

"Does it look like I sneezed?" He said as the other guard shrugged casually.

"Well I don't know I heard a sneeze," the guard added then hummed. "You should go see a healer."

His partner sighed getting upset.

"I didn't sneeze! I'm perfectly healthy!"

The guard snorted at his friend.

"Not anymore," he whispered to himself.

"I didn't sneeze!"

Making quick work of the guards, she placed the guard's unconscious bodies gently on the floor. Isa found her weapons on the table next to them. Grabbing her things, she placed them back into their correct holsters. Finally feeling complete again, she made sure everything was in place.

Running through the castle and avoiding the guards, she made it to the ground floor. Kneeling against the wall, she waited until some of the night patrols passed her. Isa needed to get back to Liliane.

She decided to head towards the stables.

Silently running across the courtyard of the front of the castle, she managed to find the royal stables.

Covering up her mouth from a deep guttural cough, Isa opened the stall as a cremello warhorse stallion lifted his head from his hay and looked at her curiously with ears perked forward. He looked a lot like the horses she had been trained to ride and handle through the cavalry, so she grinned as she entered his stall. Built to carry heavy armor, the stallion kept munching as his long white mane hung over the crest of muscle on his neck.

"I need a ride. Do you think you could help me?" Isa asked as she approached the horse its eyes a piercing arctic blue.

"*As you wish.*" The stallion replied as Isa smiled patting his neck.

With the horse's permission, Isa grabbed a bit of his mane as she swiftly mounted onto his bare back. Once she was comfortable, she kicked him forward and led them both outside into the night.

"Orion. Orion. Orion! Wake up!"

Orion sat up quickly.

"What is it, Benjamin?" He asked his good friend.

Benjamin was a cousin of the royal family and had taken up the job of learning and helping Orion with his duties while he was staying in Deval. He had dark brown skin, green eyes, and a head of black hair even more curlier and frizzier than Orion's.

"I was bringing breakfast down to her this morning and there was a panic in the prisons. They found the prison guards unconscious and she wasn't in her cell, and one of the horses from the stables had been taken. I didn't know what to do, so I came immediately to you!" Benjamin blurted out in one breath.

Orion rubbed his eyes as he tried to calm his cousin down. He had entrusted the job of keeping an eye on Isa to Benjamin when Orion couldn't do it. And it seemed that Benjamin had taken his job very seriously.

"She's escaped, Orion," Benjamin said more calmly regaining his breathing. Orion sighed as he rubbed his forehead. He should have seen this coming.

Orion ran his hands through his hair and then wiped

his face.

"Alright, don't tell anyone where I am going. Bring me, Nova."

---

Orion had an idea where Isa was heading to. She had probably escaped in the middle of the night and he knew that she wouldn't have wanted to exhaust the animal.

Orion refused to bring anyone with him and he was determined to find her.

He rode throughout the day but stopped to make camp and let his horse rest. Nova was a pure black mare that was a birthday gift from his parents.

Orion poked at the fire as Nova grazed trying to find little shrubs from within the dirt ground of the forest. Placing his arm on his leg, he rested his head on his hand. Orion looked across the fire and then next to him disappointed not having Isa there.

"It's so lonely, Nova," he said to her as she lifted her head at her name. She snorted, shaking her head and flicking her tail as she went back to eating.

Orion looked up at the sky. The stars were shining

brightly and he wondered if Isa had made it back to Liliane safely.

"Goodnight, Nova," Orion said to her, but silence was all he heard. Sighing, he walked over to lay down and closed his eyes.

The following morning, Orion and Nova were up early and back on the road. As he tugged on the reins, he turned Nova south following the dirt road towards Liliane.

<hr>

"Orion, I have no idea where she is, I'm sorry. Usually, when people come here, they are asking about Victoria's whereabouts. Why are you looking for her anyway? She was with you last time we saw her," Laura added.

Orion sighed deciding whether to tell Laura what had happened.

"She was arrested when we got to Deval and she managed to escape."

"Arrested? What?"

Orion raised his eyebrows at Laura's confusion. So, she wasn't aware of Isa's past then and Orion wasn't going to tell her without Isa's permission. Feeling defeated, Orion looked at the ground.

"Well, if she ever makes it back here, I'll let you know," Laura said in understanding, directing Orion out.

*Next, the orphanage,* he thought even more determined.

# CHAPTER 7

Orion halted Nova in front of the orphanage. Taking a deep breath, he hoped that Isa would be there as he knocked on the door with urgency.

Footsteps were heard as Ms. Whittle opened the door and didn't seem surprised to find Orion standing there. She watched him curiously until Orion spoke.

"I need to find-."

"Shush. Follow me."

Ms. Whittle opened the door for him as Orion stepped through. The inside of the orphanage was modest but brightly colored as portraits of different children hung across all the wooden walls.

"Come," she commanded gesturing for him to follow her.

The floorboards creaked underneath them as she led him up the big staircase. The stairs and floor were decorated with an old red carpet that had been worn down from years of children running around the place.

As Ms. Whittle led Orion through the hallway, he glanced at some of the portraits that hung across the walls. Suddenly, his eyes stopped at one. It was Isa's. Her cheeks were rosy and round with youth as the big toothy smile made Orion grin to himself.

Hearing a cough, he caught himself and turned towards Ms. Whittle. Down the hallway, Ms. Whittle had come to the last door. Looking at Orion, she hesitated a little bit before opening the door. Pausing and taking a deep breath, he finally stepped into the room.

Ayden screeched at Orion as Isa lay on a small bed sleeping. A short light brown-haired girl sat in a chair next to Isa wiping a wet towel across her forehead.

Orion slowly stepped closer to her bed as he noticed Isa's pale bruised face.

"How did this happen?" Orion asked concerned as he grasped Isa's hand from underneath the blankets. Her skin burned hot against his.

Ms. Whittle noticed immediately and smiled softly.

"She came to the orphanage last night falling off her

horse with fever," Ms. Whittle muttered to herself before she turned to Orion. "But I thought she was with you. What happened?"

Orion shook his head turning towards Ms. Whittle.

"She was arrested when we arrived at Deval. The guards took her to the dungeons and no one listened to me when I pleaded for her release."

Ms. Whittle crossed her arms but seemed to understand.

"And so you came to find her then?" She asked. Orion nodded sitting silently watching Isa. Ms. Whittle sighed apologetically as she came and sat down on the bed next to Isa's covered legs. Orion turned his head to look at her. Ms. Whittle hesitated gently patting one of Isa's legs before she spoke.

"My dear, I'm not sure if Isa told you much about her life. Her mother gave birth to her in this orphanage and died here. She never knew who her father was. Isa doesn't like talking about her time in Deval. So many things happened there, and it all started because she wanted to help the orphanage. I regret letting her sign up for the royal forces. But I must ask, who was the one that did this to her?" Ms. Whittle asked.

"General Adrastus."

"Cruel man," Ms. Whittle huffed. He had known the General for a while and he had never seen the General out of terms before. Orion started to question himself, but Ms. Whittle interrupted those thoughts.

"Ever since she was released from service, he has been going out of his way to threaten and intimidate her. I suspected that he loathed that she managed to come back alive from that mission and receive a medal of honor from the King," Ms. Whittle paused. She watched Orion, but he didn't react as he kept his focus on Isa. She continued.

"Did you know that he refused to send out a rescue mission? He left her and his men to die." Orion looked up shocked.

He couldn't believe it. *Why would the General risk his forces so carelessly like that? Does my father know about this?*

"I believe he was and currently is scared that she will one day take over his position at the castle," Ms. Whittle said noticing Orion's confused face.

Orion didn't say anything but turned to look at Isa softly.

*If I had known that Isa's safety was at risk, her plan, I would have never let her step foot in Deval. How long did she have to deal with all of this?*

Orion was silent thinking as Ms. Whittle sat up from the bed and patted his shoulder bringing him out of his thoughts as she turned to leave.

"But for now, the best thing she needs is rest."

Orion nodded agreeing with Ms. Whittle.

Feeling a damp towel on her forehead, Isa groggily woke up as her eyes adjusted to the all-familiar ceiling. Her eyes adjusted as the figure above slowly focused into Orion.

"Orion?" Isa whispered.

Grinning happy to see him, she was glad that he had come all this way.

"You came to find me?" She asked as she coughed out again.

Orion slumped into the chair next to Isa and crossed his arms. She noticed that he wasn't wearing his usual black leather gear, but instead a modest loose white shirt and brown pants.

"Of course, I did," Orion said softly like it was the most obvious thing in the world.

Looking up at the ceiling, Isa relaxed as the cool water traveled down her face. Her eyes closed bringing her back into the darkness.

---

Isa had no idea how much time had passed but the last thing she could remember was waking up and seeing Orion helping nurse her back to health. She looked around and saw his sleeping form on the bed next to her covered legs. Using his arms as a cushion for his head, he looked peaceful as his back moved up and down slowly with his breathing. Isa smiled to herself; he had come all this way just to find her. Wanting to reach out to him, Isa was interrupted.

"You must have made a good impression on the Prince." Ms. Whittle stood at the doorway with her arms crossed.

"You knew?" Isa questioned.

"Of course, dear. When you've lived as long as I have, you just know these things, but I'm surprised you didn't,"

Ms. Whittle chuckled as Isa followed suit, but she stopped pressing a hand to her chest.

"How long have I been out for?"

"A couple of days. Poor guy. Orion wouldn't leave your side at all during that time," Ms. Whittle told her as Isa turned down to look at her hands that had gripped her blankets.

"He likes you; you know that?" Ms. Whittle said.

"I doubt that."

It was Ms. Whittle's turn to laugh at Isa's comment.

"Think about it."

Ms. Whittle left the doorway leaving Isa to her thoughts. Plopping back down on her bed, she sighed as she stared up at the ceiling. Feeling her cheeks heat up, she covered her hands over her face. Not feeling satisfied, she grabbed her pillow from underneath her head and pressed her face against it.

Isa was used to people usually perusing Victoria, not her. *What did the Prince see in me? Maybe he felt bad about what had happened in the capital.*

"Isa?" Orion's muffled voice called out to her, interrupting her thoughts. She kept the pillow against her face despite the dull ache from her injuries.

"What are you doing under there?" He chuckled as Isa could feel Orion's hands gently lift the pillow from her face. His smiling face appeared from the side of her pillow. As she watched Orion's expression, Isa was starting to think what Ms. Whittle had told her was true.

No one had ever looked at her like that.

"Why did you come, Orion?" Isa said as she pulled the pillow down so she could hug it to her chest feeling a little self-conscious and exposed.

"I wanted to come and apologize-," Orion started as he sat down in the chair next to her, but Isa interrupted him.

"That's what you said in the dungeons," she said seriously.

"So, you were listening to me then?"

Orion sighed crossing his arms and legs leaning back into the chair.

"I didn't know this would happen to you and if I did, I would have done everything I could to prevented it." Orion finished looking up at Isa's face.

"The guards, the General, they humiliated me," Isa whispered pointing to herself as Orion reached over to gently place a hand on her shoulder staring into her dark eyes.

"I know, I know, and I'm so sorry for that. I'm sorry for everything," Orion said slowly sitting back down as Isa calmed her breathing.

"Even though you didn't tell me you were the Prince?" She asked. Orion flinched a little at her words looking down at the ground in guilt.

"I didn't tell you so that you wouldn't judge me. I know how you feel about Amarantha and I's situation." Orion looked up into Isa's dark eyes hoping that she would forgive him.

"Why did you think I would judge you? Just because you're a royal?" She paused.

"Is that why you never told me anything about yourself?" Isa said as Orion turned his head to the side embarrassed.

"Orion?" Isa asked softly making Orion turn back to her.

"If you would have told me before, then at least you wouldn't be keeping things away from me and I would have learned things about the real you," Isa reassured him, but he sighed shaking his head a little.

"Even though I am the Prince that Amarantha is engaged to? And that I've barely come out of Deval?"

"You can't control where you were born or what family you were born into," Isa paused. "I am sorry too. I'm sorry to have led you astray like that," she apologized. "Also, as far as the engagement part goes, 'was' is probably more accurate."

They both gave each other a small grin.

"I'll take you to Amarantha this time," Isa grinned as Orion looked up at her.

"Really?" Orion raised an eyebrow in doubt. Isa rolled her eyes.

"I will take you to her," Isa said jokingly as Orion nodded.

Reaching to push some stray hair away from Isa's face, he made sure that she was covered by her blankets and comfortable in bed. Isa froze a little shocked by the attention he was giving her.

As Isa rearranged herself under her covers, Orion started to walk towards the door to leave. As he reached the door, he paused turning over his shoulder to look at her.

With his hand on the doorknob, Orion grinned one last time at her before opening the door and stepping out of the room.

Isa grinned.

# CHAPTER 8

Isa managed to regain her strength a few days after Orion's arrival. Thankfully, Ms. Whittle and Orion's constant care helped her recover quickly. During that time, Isa felt that something had changed within her and she could feel that every time she looked at Orion.

Ms. Whittle's words echoed in her mind.

Isa had promised Orion to take him to see Amarantha and she was planning to keep her word this time.

Ayden had told Isa that he was staying near the Silva Forest to make sure that no one from Deval would come to the orphanage. She was thankful for him being her eyes and ears in the forest.

When they were preparing for their travel to Queenside, Orion had introduced Nova to Isa. She complimented how exquisite of a horse she was and loved her shiny black coat. Nova shook her mane in thanks, loving the attention.

Finally leaving Liliane, Isa directed them east towards Queenside on her own chestnut horse she had bought named Penny. She was going to take the most direct route as they both rode next to each other in peaceful silence until Isa spoke up.

"Orion?" She said looking down at her hands that gripped the leather reins.

"Yes?" He replied worried something was wrong as he turned to look at her.

Before answering, she let out a breath, still feeling a subtle ache. Her chest was still sore, but at least she wasn't coughing as much.

Isa hesitated a bit before starting.

"I just want to say thank you for helping me. Ms. Whittle told me what you did for me." Isa waited for Orion's answer.

"Well, it was the least I could do to repay you back for the torture you had to endure at Deval," Orion whispered as he looked over to see Isa's injuries. There was still a scab over her nose, but the bandage wasn't there anymore and the bruise had healed into a little discoloration.

"Orion, I'm fine now. I'm alright," Isa stated looking at him sternly.

"Ok, I'll let it go," he said as Isa nodded happily.

"Good. Now I'll race ya!" She challenged as she kicked Penny forward into a fast canter down the long road to Queenside.

"Cheater!" Orion smirked as he kicked Nova forward to catch up with her.

———◦———

That night at their camp, Isa and Orion sat beside each other as they ate the game that Isa was able to capture. Instead of the forest, they were camping out on the open rolling plains and as the sun dropped from behind the small hills, the sky looked even more expansive than before.

Having relaxed on the flat rock, Orion was happy to travel with Isa again. But he still had some questions that needed answering.

"Why weren't you going to take me to see Amarantha?" He asked her.

"Well, simple. I didn't trust you."

Orion nodded.

"Understandable, but I can't *believe* you didn't trust me!" Orion exclaimed placing a hand over his heart jokingly and leaned in closer to her. Isa rolled her eyes nudging his shoulder, laughing at him. Seeing her smile made Orion's heart flutter as he watched her mouth crinkle in happiness. At that point, Isa knew what Ms. Whittle had told her was right. But the problem was, how did she feel?

Awkward silence filled the camp as they didn't speak or look at each other until they started to feel tired. The fire crackled in front of them and Isa watched the little sparks travel up into the sky trying to look anywhere except for at Orion.

Once they were ready to go to sleep for the night, Isa pulled out her sleeping materials but then saw Orion standing right next to her with his pack.

"What are you doing?" Isa asked crossing her arms as Orion placed his sleeping mat beside hers.

"To make sure you're actually feeling better," Orion said as he continued to unpack not seeing anything wrong.

Once they had finished unpacking, they plopped down

onto their respected mats and froze with eyes wide. Laying down next to each other, their faces were so close that their noses were almost touching.

Isa watched Orion's eyes search her own face as they stared at each other unmoving. Feeling each other breaths, they both chuckled in embarrassment as Isa turned over onto the other side of her sleeping mat covering her face with her hands.

⸻◆⸻

Isa and Orion arrived at Queenside the following day. The Jones' farm was on the outskirts of the main town. Orion noticed how different this farming town was compared to Liliane.

Riding along the stone wall, they passed by fields of cows as the orange sky lighted their way through other farms. Orion and Isa happily chatted away as she directed them through the empty dirt labyrinth of roads leading to other farms until she stopped by the gate of one of them.

"This is it," Isa pointed to the house as clanging of pots and pans was heard, then a face popped up through the kitchen window to see who was there. Gasping and grinning wide, Amarantha was the first to jump out of the house. Smiling too, Isa dismounted as Amarantha ran to hug her.

Coming out of the hug, Amarantha grinned at Isa grasping her elbows.

"Welcome back my friend, it is so good to see you." She grinned but then frowned wiggling a finger over Isa's nose. "But what happened here?"

Smiling back, Isa laughed it off.

"That's a long story for another time, but how are you Amarantha? You seem to have settled down well. You look happy."

"All thanks to you," Amarantha told her before she turned to see Orion dismount Nova behind them. Once he was on the ground, Amarantha waved and called out to him.

"Orion!" She exclaimed.

Isa watched curiously as Amarantha walked around her pulling Orion into his own bone crushing hug. Isa stood there with her eyebrows raised.

"Thank you to both of you for helping me in your own ways," Amarantha said as she glanced at each of them.

First, Amarantha turned to look at Orion.

"To Orion for helping me escape the castle," she paused as Isa looked at him shocked.

"What?" She whispered in disbelief.

"Did he not tell you Isa? Orion helped me navigate the castle and Deval so that I could escape into the forest." Amarantha's voice made Isa look back at her in shock.

*Orion had helped her? He didn't mention that part to me. So, he really was trying to make sure Amarantha was safe.* As Isa processed this, she watched him with an open mouth.

"You helped Amarantha? Why didn't you tell me?" Isa asked Orion as he looked at her shrugging his shoulders.

"You never asked."

Isa gave a hearty laugh at his comment as Orion smiled with her all the while Amarantha looked between the two of them with a slight smirk.

"Ama, what are you doing out here? It's getting cold and dark!" Quinn called out as he walked towards them.

The young farmer came up behind Amarantha placing a wool shawl over her shoulders before wrapping a hand around her waist. Feeling Quinn beside her, Amarantha tightened the shawl around herself grinning up at him and stepped back into his arms.

"Are you guys-," Isa asked before Amarantha answered excitedly nodding her head as she raised her right arm.

"Mhm, we got married! Just a couple of weeks ago too!"

"Congratulations," Orion said smiling as he reached over to shake hands with Quinn introducing himself. With their introductions, Amarantha came up to stand beside Isa again.

"Isa," she said bringing Isa out of her daze. "Beth wants to talk to you about arrangements for this upcoming winter. Quinn, go tell Beth that Isa is here," Amarantha finished turning to Quinn as Orion turned around to look at them.

"Of course, my desert flower," Quinn answered stepping towards Amarantha to give her a kiss before he gestured for Isa to follow him to the front of the house.

As Quinn and Isa walked to the front of the stone home, Orion followed her with his eyes. Quinn leaned around the corner of the door calling out to Beth as she appeared in the doorway. Noticing Isa, Beth grinned hugging her as a mother would do.

"I see the way you look at her Orion and I am happy for you." Amarantha stood beside him as she spoke up to him, interrupting his focus for a second. Turning towards the princess, Orion shook his head realizing what he was doing.

"I don't know, Amarantha," he said waving her off and scratching his head. She couldn't help but notice the soft red coloration across his face.

"Trust me Orion she most likely feels the same way," she said crossing her arms. Hearing Isa laugh from behind Amarantha, Orion glanced at her again sighing.

"How do you know?" He asked, keeping his focus on Isa.

"We women know this kind of thing," Amarantha smiled patting his shoulder before turning serious.

"I think she will be better for Atalia more than I would have ever been." Amarantha said as she moved to stand at Orion's side again watching Quinn, Isa, and Beth talk to each other.

"You were raised to be a queen Amarantha," Orion said but it seemed that she had already made up her mind.

"Isa already has the respect from all the citizens of

Atalia. She is admired, Orion. She helped the Jones' and other families here in Queenside countless times, and they have helped her," Amarantha paused.

"Isa gave them the land she was awarded by your father. Ever since then, she has brought them food during particularly hard winters, and in the spring time, she's made sure the birds helped keep all the pesky insects away from the crops. And of course, she helped me find a home. She listens and she assists."

Orion didn't say anything after her comment.

"Ama! You are needed." Quinn waved to Amarantha ending their conservation.

"Be right there!" The Princess called out. As Amarantha turned to leave, she looked behind her at Orion again. Before he could protest, she grabbed his pale hands in her darker ones, surprising him.

"You have my blessing," she said before she released him.

"For what?" Orion crossed his arms chuckling to himself watching her walk away from him.

"Well, that's up for you to decide my friend."

Walking back to Orion, Isa looked down at the cobbled

courtyard until she came up next to Orion looking back at Amarantha and Quinn.

"I'm glad she is finally happy. Thank you for bringing me to her," Orion said as he looked at Isa next to him, who nodded and then grinned satisfied.

"Isa! Orion! You should have dinner with us!" Beth shouted across the courtyard as she waved to them. Isa stopped and turned around but before she could respond, Amarantha peaked from behind Beth.

"Even better, stay the night!' Amarantha said as Beth wholeheartedly agreed with her. Walking back up to Orion, Isa chuckled looking at him as he did the same.

"Well, whatever the princess commands," he said.

Isa laughed making Orion's chest flutter.

# CHAPTER 9

The homemade meal brought warmth back into Isa's body. She hadn't been this inclined to overeat and enjoy herself in a long time in a long time. She had also discovered that Amarantha had really found her talent in cooking. Remembering the first time Isa had dropped Amarantha off here, she found that the Princess had flourished into such an outgoing and lively person, opposite to the shy and frightened girl in the forest.

After dinner and clean up, Amarantha led both Isa and Orion up the wooden stairs to the bedrooms. The stairs creaked as they made their way up. In-between both, Amarantha had one arm wrapped around Isa and the other around Orion.

"You both can take the spare bedroom," Amarantha said as she released them walking in front to the one of the wooden doors down the hallway.

Immediately walking into the room, Isa furrowed her eyebrows.

"There's only one bed, Amarantha?" She asked confused turning around to see Amarantha's sly smile.

"We are but humble modest folks, Isa." Amarantha raised an eyebrow innocently before closing the door behind them.

Damnit Amarantha.

"I can sleep on the floor," Orion started trying to get the fire going but Isa interrupted him.

"Orion, I know you haven't slept well in a while. We can share. Just be aware that if you so much as try to hug me in your sleep your dead." Isa pointed at him trying to look serious, but she couldn't help the small grin.

"I wouldn't expect any less," Orion laughed standing up to face her as he crossed his arms.

Once the household had turned quiet and still, Isa laid in bed. Listening as everyone turned in for the night, she turned to her side in the bed, facing away from Orion. After a couple of seconds of listening to her heartbeat, she opened her mouth.

"Orion? Are you awake?" Isa whispered as she kept

facing the wall at the edge of the bed.

"Everything ok?" He whispered back as he moved around under the covers. Sighing, Isa tuned around onto her other side to face him. Despite the darkness in the room, she could still see Orion's face.

"I'm just glad Amarantha is happy in her new home," Isa whispered, reaching a hand underneath the pillow to prop her head up.

"Me too," Orion smiled agreeing with her.

"Something else bothering you?" He whispered as she sighed looking up at him.

"What about her parents? How do you think they would feel about their daughter, that was promised to you, marrying a commoner?" Isa sighed as she turned over onto her back to look up at the ceiling placing an arm over her stomach. Sighing, Orion did the same as they both looked up at the wooden beamed ceiling.

"Let's deal with that when we get back to Deval," Orion said as Isa turned her head to the side to look at him furrowing her eyebrows.

"We?" Isa sat up in bed, her focus on him. Orion sighed as he did the same leaning against his elbow to face her.

"I want you to come back with me to Deval. I want my father to issue *you* a full pardon. And I want him to hear what you know about the deaths that have been happening," he started.

"I want him to give you full diplomatic immunity. I don't want you to feel unsafe every time you step foot into the capital."

She had never seen him that serious before as Isa looked at him, ready to talk.

"When I first joined the special forces, your father had sent us out on a secret undercover quest into Endrancia since we were still at war with them. Once we got there, we did our intelligence scouting, reporting any information we could find directly back to the General and your father. After about a month of gathering intel, one of our messengers was captured and killed on his way to us. Since he was intercepted, we didn't receive the new orders, so we were ambushed, captured, and imprisoned. They took us to an underground prison facility in the middle of the city which had a reputation for being one of the worse prisons in Endrancia."

It was obviously a painful memory for her as Orion

stayed silent. Isa continued.

"They tortured me for hours just for the little bits of information I held. It was horrible and I didn't know what to do. The only thing I could do was to take the pain so that they wouldn't hurt anyone else. When I didn't cooperate, they chained me up and whipped me."

Orion was about to tell her that she didn't need to continue as she wiped her eyes taking a deep breath.

"For a week I was tied up in that cell with no food and bare minimum water, but it felt longer than that. I was so weak and tired that I was barely able to speak so they threw me into the prison area with everyone else. I was worried that they might sell me as a slave. My wounds weren't healing, so I was brought to the prison doctor, Najia. After Ms. Whittle, she was the kindest and bravest woman I had ever known. She healed my wounds and I owe my entire life to her." Isa grinned a bit as she regained her composure remembering her friend.

"As I recovered, I started to scout out the area to possibly escape."

*Isa didn't know that her commander had refused to lead a rescue mission then,* Orion thought as he listened to Isa's story, her eyes glossy with unshed tears.

"Another month passed, and my back was pretty much healed at that point, so I was fit to fight again. My team and I were able to gain some allies within that prison. So, we led a prison uprising. Most of the men there were Atalian soldiers or Endrancian thieves. While the guards were distracted with angry prisoners and an army of small rodents, courtesy of yours truly, we all walked right out of that prison and back into the city. But there was one person I couldn't save," Isa whispered looking down at the white bed sheets.

"Who?" Orion asked quietly.

Isa sighed before looking back up to him.

"When I turned back to see if everyone had made it out, I didn't know that some of the prison wardens had captured Najia. It was my fault. They slit her throat." Isa closed her eyes remembering the person she owed her life to. She would never be able to repay her for what she did.

"It felt like my body was on fire as my blood rushed through me." Isa paused gulping. "Something fueled inside me, all I remember was seeing red. But before I could stop myself, I realized that I had killed those guards mercilessly for what they did to Najia. I had no remorse for their lives, I had become a monster by fighting those monsters."

Isa paused as she shifted around in bed a little bit.

"I gathered myself leading everyone out of Endrancia and back into Atalia. As you know from there, I was given the medal of honor for what I did. My team then demanded that I get prompted to the lieutenant position, which I declined," Isa said as she chuckled to herself.

"All I kept thinking about was that Najia really deserved this recognition, not me. I vowed to never take another innocent person's life mercilessly ever again and do as much as I can to help people," she paused finally looking up at Orion.

"The day before I was about to leave for Liliane, General Adrastus threatened me."

Isa swallowed.

"Are you scared that something worse would happen to you if you ever stepped into Deval again?" Orion asked softly.

"I don't want to fight him or anyone at the castle. I just want peace and a chance to help my people."

"I promise you will never be hurt," Orion told her.

Trying to comfort her, Orion reached over and grasped her shoulders making her turn to face him. Orion kept his warm hands on her shoulders.

"I will protect you, and don't worry about General Adrastus. Once my father grants you clemency, you will be protected. And you can plead to my father about the people in Liliane."

Hesitating to see if Isa would object, Orion slowly cupped her cheeks with his hands being careful of her bruise. Watching him, Isa's heart thumped against her chest so hard that she swore that Orion could hear it. He only softly grinned at her as she stared at him accepting his comforting touch against her face.

"Come back to Deval, Isa. Help your people and help me convince Amarantha's parents that she is happy, married and starting a new life in Atalia. You can help me make them understand," he whispered.

Maybe in Deval, she can find the answers to the strange darkness that had plagued Liliane. There would be more resources for her in the capital and with Orion, she would have full access to whatever she needed.

Clearing her throat, she answered.

"I will go with you."

---

"Shush! Quiet!"

Giggles emerged from the silence as the oldest of the group, Victoria, quieted the little girls. She had been dying to try out this new spell she had acquired from one of her schoolmates in town.

In the shared girls' dormitory in the small town of Liliane, all the youngsters in the girl's dorm from ages five to sixteen had downed their blankets and were huddled in the middle of the brick-and-stone room. Their wooden bunk beds surrounded them empty and dark as the one big fireplace crackled with heat casting their shadows behind them. Each girl grabbed a candle from around the room and used the dying fire to light their wax stick.

Sitting down on the floor in a circle, all the girls had eagerly jumped off their bunks and onto the wooden floors, adrenaline rushing through them, fearful of being caught. Their cheeks were red with excitement for what they were about to do.

Victoria finally sat down with her own flickering candle in one hand and another resting on top of her knee casually as she turned to one of the fifteen-year-old ginger-haired girls in the room, Laura. The freckles on her pale complexion could barely be seen from the candlelight.

"You first Laura, wish into the candle and blow it out when you're done!" Victoria instructed gesturing towards her. The girls all giggled again bouncing in excitement.

But Laura hesitated as she swallowed.

"I don't know Victoria. Is this safe? We shouldn't be using magic so lightly. Plus can we even trust this 'friend' of yours?" Laura questioned whispering too anxious as Victoria scuffed rolling her hazel eyes.

"Don't worry, I've done it a million times already," Victoria reassured the girl waving her off. Isa, with big brown eyes wide in wonder and cheeks round with youth, sat on Victoria's opposite side waiting patiently for Laura to go.

"My dream boy will be . . . let's see . . .," Laura thought out loud as Victoria scuffed.

"Any day now." Victoria raised her eyebrows at Laura as Isa tried to hide her giggle. Laura opened her mouth protesting Victoria's impatience.

"As I was saying, my dream boy will have wonderful green eyes that sparkle, dark hair like the night sky, and would love to eat any food I cook," Laura added at the end whispering into her candle. Then, she blew it out. Once Laura was done with her wish, the other girls each went around the circle wishing for their ideal future husband.

Finally, it was Victoria's turn. She had been eyeing each girl waiting for her chance to wish into the candle.

"Well, my perfect man ... hm. Well, I want him to be exotic, Atalian men are too bland for my taste. Oh, he should be able to take a joke or too and be able to handle all of me-," Victoria started leaning back on her hand and thinking dramatically staging up for the other girls.

"I don't think there is a man anywhere like that."

All the girls giggled at Abbie's comment. Victoria turned her head and pouted at her.

"No one asked you, Abbie." Victoria stuck her tongue out at the short light brown-haired girl. More giggles echoed around the room as the fire sparked behind them.

"Anyway, what about you, Isa?" Victoria noticed the last girl to go and nudged the other fifteen-year-old sitting next to her. Shyly, she looked up surprised, and found many eyes on her. Gulping nervously, Isa looked at all the invested and intrigued eyes before speaking.

"I wish for him to be kind and love me no matter what even if I don't have any family. I want him to have a love of adventure so that we can travel everywhere on the continent. And I want him to be a Prince of some far-off kingdom so we can ride off together into the far unknown," Isa finished as she closed her eyes and then blew out her candle.

As she opened her eyes again, she watched as the last bits of the flames rose into the air and disappeared. Silence followed her wish, until giggles picked up again. Confused, Isa watched the girls whisper to each other feeling like she had said something wrong.

Feeling a pat on her shoulder, Isa turned to Abbie.

"That's asking a little too much, Isa," she said apologetically. Victoria pushed Abbie away wrapping an arm around Isa's shoulders.

"Abbie don't start-," Victoria started but she was interrupted.

"Your wish has to be real," another girl added as Isa

looked around the room at the others. Her cheeks heated up in embarrassment.

"But why not? It's my wish," Isa said paying no mind to the other girls laughing and commenting about how her wish would never come true, but that was all part of the fun. Isa had a gut feeling that her wish would someday come true, but with all of the girls' glances and laughter, she doubted herself.

"Only Princesses get to be with Princes," another girl added which made Isa look down at the wooden floor dropping her candle into her lap.

Maybe she was right. She wasn't a Princess; she didn't even know who her real family was. She didn't even know her full name.

She wasn't anyone special.

Suddenly, Victoria heard footsteps and panicked, rushing the girls back into their bunk beds. Everyone scurried and climbed to their appropriate beds as Isa jumped back underneath her covers. She looked up at the ceiling in thought.

*I wish.*

# CHAPTER 10

The fields were still misty and foggy from the morning dew as Amarantha helped them pack some food for the journey. She smiled at their receding forms before she too got ready for another day of harvesting.

As they traveled along the main road, Orion acknowledged the farmers and merchants that passed by in their carriages as Isa kept to herself. Orion seemed happy to have Isa accompany him back to Deval again. He whistled to himself silently, which made her smile but she was grateful for the relaxing ride.

Camping on the outskirts of the forest in the night was peaceful as Orion once again placed his sleeping mat next to Isa who chuckled at him. As they lay on their backs watching the stars after dinner, Orion listened to Isa's soft breathing. Orion turned his head to look at her. Watching her eyes examining the stars above them, he smiled gently at her seeing the light of the fire illuminate her face as small scars he hadn't notice before. He looked back up to her eyes before he asked Isa the question he had on the back of his mind.

"Why did you help Amarantha?" He asked out of nowhere.

"What do you mean?" Isa asked her eyes flickering between his own.

"I mean the way you were treated in Endrancia. Why did you help a Princess? A royal?"

Crossing her legs over her ankles, Isa placed her hands on her stomach before continuing.

"I thought of Najia. I wanted to save Amarantha and protect her the way I could not do with Najia," she ended.

Sighing, Orion rolled over onto his side and watched the fire die down as he closed his eyes. Finally hearing that he had stopped moving and his breathing had slowed down, Isa turned over her shoulder at him before siting up with her bow and arrows in hand. Even with the soft glow of the dying fire, she was able to make her way around the forest.

Finding a nice small clearing a little way away from

camp, she stood in the middle of the trees, nocked an arrow, pulled back on the bow string, and released it into a tree trunk. Three more arrows flew in rapid succession each near each other in the bark of the tree. Once she was empty, Isa walked over to get her arrows back. As she pulled the arrows out of the tree, Isa heard a flap of wings as Ayden perched on top of a nearby branch and followed her walk back to her spot and nock more arrows.

*"Worried?"* Ayden questioned as Isa sighed releasing another arrow. She waited until the arrow stuck into the tree before answering.

"Orion is taking me back to Deval," Isa said holding an arrow before turning to Ayden who flapped his wings at her.

*"Maybe that's not a bad thing,"* he said.

"Are you on Orion's side?" She released the arrow and with a thunk, hit the tree in front of her.

*"Well I like him. But really, why not? This might be your chance to see the King and at least you won't be alone this time."*

Isa leaned against her bow. She knew that Ayden did make a good point.

"True. Orion promised to look out for me, but he's the future King of Atalia. What would people think about that? What about once he ascends the throne?" Isa quickly lifted her bow again nocking an arrow and pulled back on the bow string twisting her waist to release it into a different tree.

*"You won't be hurt."* Isa sighed looking down at the forest floor at Ayden's comment.

"How do you know that?" She whispered at Ayden.

*"Orion won't let that happen."*

"I don't know Ayden."

*"You must start trusting people again Isa,"* Ayden paused. *"He likes you too, you know."*

At his words, Isa turned towards him and could hear the smirk in Ayden's voice.

*"Well, you'll have to figure that out before you get to Deval. You deserve this."*

"Speaking of Deval, I need you to do something for me," Isa asked, but Ayden was silent as he titled his head again waiting for her to continue.

"Go to Liliane. I need someone I can trust to make sure that no one puts the orphanage in danger while I'm away."

Isa leaned against her bow her muscles aching ready for sleep. Looking up at the sky above her, the stars twinkled brightly down at her. Maybe this would really give her a chance to make peace and amends with what she had to go through in the capital.

As the trees around her went silent again, Isa moved some forest dirt around with her boot as she thought about what Ayden had told her. *What was his real motive in bringing her to Deval? A job perhaps?* She thought. Start a new life instead of hunting in the forest all the time selling carcasses.

She could feel the forest going to sleep around her as she walked back to the dying fire of their camp.

As she made her way back, she passed by Orion who looked at peace. Isa smiled gently to herself as she lied down facing him. It was then that Isa realized that she could watch him for hours. His chest moved up and down to his breathing.

Feeling safe with his presence next to her, Isa smiled.

⸻◦○◦⸻

As they rode through the main town passing underneath

the iron gate of Deval, Isa recognized the looming stone castle on top of the hill by the edge of the steep cliff. The lake crashed against the rocky side and the big plains roamed on the other sides of the city. The safety of the forest loomed behind them as the gates closed sealing them inside. Deval was busy as usual as people stepped to the side bowing as Orion rode through.

Isa didn't know what to do as people noticed her beside the Prince. She was used to being invisible not on full display in front of the people.

Trying at least to look friendly, Isa awkwardly smiled and waved at the children before their mothers dragged them away from the road.

Once Isa and Orion made it to the main inner gates of the castle, the guards opened it for the both of them. Isa stopped her horse as stable boys rushed to take their horses after they dismounted.

A boy, around Isa's age, jumped out from the side doors of the castle entrance and went straight towards them. Green eyes crinkled in happiness in seeing Orion as his tight black curls bounced as he ran towards them. Watching him, Isa stayed silent but observant as Orion stepped to ingulf him in a hug. Orion patted his back in excitement as the boy did the same to Orion.

"Isa this is my cousin and friend, Benjamin, Duke of Camoora," Orion said. Immediately, Benjamin bowed towards her, and she looked at him in shock not expecting this.

"You can call me Benjamin. Orion has told me so much about you," Benjamin said as he got up from the bow and reached a light brown hand towards Isa to shake.

"All good things, I hope. Nice to meet you, Benjamin," Isa smiled accepting his hand trying to be polite. Benjamin chuckled.

"Yes, Orion wouldn't stop talking about you," he said smiling as he scratched the back of his head.

"Oh! I also brought you food when you were in the prison-," Benjamin started but he was interrupted by Orion patting his shoulder.

"Please, Ben, let's not talk about that shall we." Orion glanced at Isa giving her a small smile.

"Do you know where my parents are?" Orion asked clapping his hands together. Isa's heart spiked.

"Your father is in his study, and I have no idea where

your mother is," Benjamin answered. The prince nodded.

"Ok, can you let them know we are here?" Orion asked. Benjamin smiled happily and nodded looking between Isa and Orion.

"Of course, Orion. Nice to meet you, Isa," Benjamin waved at her before he ran back into the castle. Smiling at his receding form, Isa weakly waved back at him. Once he was out of sight, she turned towards Orion, who looked down at her.

"Nice kid," Isa said as Orion chuckled at her comment.

"Yes, quite the energetic person too. He lost his parents when he was young and was put into his dukedom very young. He is here in Atalia to learn and help me prepare to rule. He definitely keeps me on my toes."

They both stepped inside the great hall and it was still as beautiful as the last time she had first stepped into the throne room.  The two thrones carved into the marble platform still lay before them as Isa looked around again Orion watching her. He was glad that she was able to come here without being too afraid, but then she could be hiding it well.

Suddenly, squeals and screams of the ladies of the court were heard as they all rounded the corner from another part of the castle.

Their target: Isa.

Shocked, Isa's eyes widened as the group of ladies grasped her arms to drag her away from Orion before she could do anything about it.

"Orion! What is this? I think this may be scarier than the dungeons!" Isa shouted at Orion, who just stood there clearly entertained.

"We've been expecting you!" One of the girls shouted as they all giggled to themselves continuing to drag Isa away.

Orion took in the comforting smell of the great hall before he heard the smooth and rhythmic footsteps of his mother as she rounded the corner with Benjamin at her side. Regal as ever she presented herself with confidence and calm as she noticed Orion standing alone.

"Mother?" Orion paused as he crossed his arms at his mother as she approached him.

"All the girls were waiting to capture your friend."

In another room of the castle, Isa was being pampered by all the girls. They pushed each other around trying to get to Isa. So many arms and hands were touching her but Isa was too tired to care.

As they stripped her, some of the ladies had to cover sharp breaths over her scars on her back, but they didn't say anything. The ladies kept going as they bathed her and took out her braids.

She felt light and clean for the first time in a while.

"You're very lucky." A slender platinum blonde haired girl told Isa as she brushed out Isa's now wavy dark hair.

Isa was silent in her chair. The girl noticed her silence before she introduced herself looking at Isa through the mirror.

"I'm Tania," she said as Isa smiled politely at her.

"Isa."

"I know." Tania smiled jokingly at her as she kept combing through Isa's hair. Isa nodded as Tania continued to brush through her dark waves.

"So, what are you preparing me for exactly?" Isa asked a bit confused.

"Dinner with the royal family of course."

Isa turned in her seat panicking.

"What? So soon?"

"Don't worry, Isa, we will help you look presentable," Tania said patting her shoulders as Isa turned back around towards the vanity.

From behind Isa, the girls presented her with a burgundy-colored dress with black and gold embroidery all around the fabric.

Once they were done, some girls presented a full body mirror to Isa, who stood up from the chair and finally looked at herself. She could tell it was herself, but different.

Good different.

"Now you're finally ready," Tania said as she stepped back to look at Isa.

"I don't know if I can do this," Isa whispered clasping her hands in front of her.

"Yes, you can. You are one of us now," Tania finished.

*Could I face the King again? Could I face Orion looking like this? What would he think about seeing me like this? Would he like it?* Before she could say anything, Isa was whisked away again, but this time to the outside of the castle.

Leading Isa away, the girls dragged her to the castle

gardens where trimmed bushes and intricate fountains were scattered across the green landscape.

"Hey!" Isa shouted trying to gain someone's attention.

She was alone.

"Isa?"

She turned towards Orion's voice as he stood in front of her his eyes wide as a small smile creeped on to his face. Orion had changed his clothes too. He had cleaned up very well Isa thought as she too looked at him.

"Wow, you look-," Orion began not taking his eyes off her, but Isa cut him off.

"Different, I know," Isa interrupted as she grabbed the dress fabric and moved it around twirling herself.

"I was going to say beautiful," Orion whispered as he reached a hand for her to take. "You ready?"

Isa looked down at his outstretched hand waiting, hoping, there for her to take.

Taking a deep breath, she nodded.

"Ready as I'll ever be," Isa said as she placed her hand in his.

Orion gently closed his fingers around her hand and pulled her towards him. Once he had her hand, he placed it around his arm as Orion led her from the gardens and back into the castle.

# CHAPTER 11

As Isa and Orion walked into the royal family's private dining room, she noticed the rectangular long table, antlers decorating the stone walls. The King and Queen both turned to greet them.

From what she knew, a lot of people liked the Queen but that was also because no one knew a lot about her either. It was all rumor for the most part. But as Isa locked eyes with Orion's mother, something in the Queen's face made Isa question herself.

The Queen almost seemed stunned as she stepped forward taking Isa's hand from Orion's arm. Orion's mother kissed both of her cheeks like a close friend.

"Welcome, Isa. Thank you for joining us for dinner. Come sit down next to me." Orion's mother spoke eloquently and softly leading her to the dining table.

"Orion told us that your name is Isa. What is your

family crest?" The Queen asked.

"I don't know your Majesty." Isa shook her head sitting down. The Queen looked at her curiously.

"You do not know?"

"I don't have a last name," Isa replied quietly. The Queen turned to Orion who had seated himself down next to Isa.

"She does not have a last name?" She asked her son. Isa watched their interaction trying to keep a straight face.

"Orion told us that you were in the royal cavalry?" The King asked as Isa turned towards him.

"Yes, your Majesty and then I was accepted into the special forces."

"It must have been challenging as a young woman to be in the army," The Queen asked.

"I was proud to serve my kingdom," Isa stated. The Queen's eyes searched Isa's face, analyzing her.

"Isa, I heard from Lord Byran that his carriage was looted on the way to the capital. How does one go from receiving a medal of honor to robbing nobles for money? Are things that troublesome for my people out there right now?" The King clasped his hands in front of him.

"Your Majesty, I didn't rob his carriage for money. Liliane, the village where I grew up has been plagued by some evil darkness. I witnessed many deaths in the last month. They all seem to be from a dark magic poison. My people, children, are dying. My intention was to use the money for medicine and protection."

The King combed through his beard.

"Father, believe me. I was there. I witnessed one of these deaths," Orion spoke up as Isa looked at him.

"And I ask you to give Isa royal protection and immunity, while she is here in the castle."

The King paused watching Orion before turning back to Isa.

"Alright, I will grant you immunity," he continued. "And I will send healers and soldiers to Liliane. My advisors will send out notices to all of the villages so that they can be aware of the situation."

The weight on Isa's shoulders lifted. But before she could reply, General Adrastus burst through the doors.

"Intruder in the castle!"

Isa tensed up. Reaching under her dress, she tried to find her dagger. Orion stopped her placing his hand on top of hers. Her heart skipped a beat.

"Intruder? Is the castle under attack, General? Compose yourself, we have a guest in our castle today."

General Adrastus noticed Isa sitting at the table watching him sternly as he put on a fake smile.

"Your Majesty, I apologize it was a false alarm," he whispered staring at Isa. That's when she realized that she would never be safe as long as General Adrastus was still in the castle.

After the General left the dining room, Orion's mother turned to Isa.

"Isa, you must join me tomorrow for tea with the ladies of the court," the Queen said.

"Of course, your Majesty," Isa answered as she glanced at Orion who nodded slightly at her.

"Isa and I would like to retire to our rooms," Orion said as he stood up to stand behind Isa's chair.

His parents nodded their head saying their goodbye's as the pair walked out of the dining room.

Coming up to their bedrooms, Orion had made sure the room next to his was prepared for Isa. Orion wanted to make sure that Isa would feel safe while here in the castle.

"Guards will be posted outside your room."

"Thank you, Orion. For what you did and for depending me," Isa said giving him a small grin as she jumped up to wrap her arms around his shoulders embracing him. Orion smiled and wrapped his arms around her too.

Once they were in heir respective rooms, Isa laid in the comfortable bed. Wanting to keep the curtains open, the moon shone through her window as she turned to her side to look at it. Despite what had happened during dinner, she felt she accomplished what she came for.

*I have immunity now and the King is sending help to the villages and towns. But what about the General?* Isa thought.

---

*Maybe the General is not the only thing I have to worry about.*

Isa watched the older ladies of the court awkwardly as they politely laughed at whatever the Queen had said. Their polite smiles, soft chuckles that meant nothing, it felt rehearsed, staged. Sitting next to Orion's mother, Isa blinked holding a cup of tea as she looked out the window at the sunny morning.

"Now ladies, Isa here has graciously agreed to join us for tea today, so let's show her some hospitality." The Queen placed a gentle hand on Isa's shoulder.

"Is Isa short for Isabelle or Isabella?" A lady across from Isa asked intrigued.

"Uh, no. Just Isa," Isa said softly still holding the teacup. She could feel the eyes all on her, watching her movements and looking at her up and down, judging. Isa felt like she was being examined, but she stayed composed.

"This is Lady Kathleen; her husband helps with the fishing exports in Atalia." The Queen told her as Isa raised her eyebrows in polite interest and smiled at the lady.

"Do you have any hobbies, Isa?" The women on the next chair over questioned. This ladies' general aura seemed the opposite of Lady Kathleen's.

"I like to hunt," Isa answered turning to her, but Lady Vivianna didn't seem pleased at all as she briefly glanced at Isa before turning back to her teacup.

"No, dear, not men sports. I mean skills every woman

should know." She took another sip of tea watching Isa almost as if testing her. Isa didn't know what she had expected her to say.

"I used to play the flute." Isa smiled awkwardly waving her hand off.

"Shame really. Did your mother not teach you anything?" Lady Vivianna asked, twirling her spoon in her teacup. Isa watched her differently now. The best thing to do was to not react and make a fool out of herself.

"My mother is dead," Isa said sternly with no emotion.

"Oh, dear that must have been difficult, I'm sorry."

"Despite never knowing  who my real family is, I received plenty of love at the orphanage," Isa said before the Queen spoke up.

"Isa here used to be in the royal cavalry under my husband. She is a brave and strong young woman who was accepted into the Special Forces in the army." Orion's mother smiled at her before looking at the ladies, hoping to move the conversation further. Looking at Orion's mother confused, Isa suddenly realized what was happening. The Queen was trying to make Isa look impressive to the ladies. But why?

"Really? How impressive!" Lady Kathleen exclaimed leaning forward in her chair again intrigued. Isa nodded ready to answer but was interrupted by Lady Vivianna.

"Did you have to go back home to help your father or brothers after the war?"

Isa kept her voice calm and collected.

"I have no family. My family has been and will always be the children from the orphanage and Ms. Whittle, the woman who raised me," Isa said as she stared at Lady Vivianna who glanced up at her, reciprocating her stare.

Isa waited until Lady Vivianna's gaze moved away from hers before she turned to the Queen.

"May I be excused? Ladies, a pleasure," Isa said standing up and walking out of the room. Orion's mother did the same following her out.

# CHAPTER 12

"You handled yourself well." The Queen told Isa catching up to her in the halls of the castle.

Isa smiled as she looked down at the red carpet beneath them.

The Queen spoke again as they continued to walk together.

"In my role as Queen, you need to show strength. Most importantly, be prepared to have your name spread," the Queen warned her. They had stopped in front of Isa's room.

"I understand, your Majesty. I welcome your advice."

Orion's mother smiled genuinely at her before turning to leave.

Isa stood in front of her door for a second too long before going into her room. Her bed had been made and the window was opening letting in the cool autumn breeze.

Seeing her hunting clothes washed and folded on the desk in the room, Isa peeled off her dress quickly. After she was done, she headed back out into the hallways of the castle with her staff on her back.

She felt like herself knowing she had her weapons with her. As she walked through the castle, she tried to find Benjamin. Isa finally found the curly haired dark skinned boy talking to a servant in the hallway. Waving to him, Isa approached him and pulled him to the side.

His green eyes widened in worry.

"I need your help, Benjamin."

"Is everything, alright? Do I need to find Orion?" He asked glancing behind her before Isa held her hand up to his face, silencing him.

"No! No, I'm fine," she chuckled. "I need to know where the private training grounds are."

Benjamin nodded and guided Isa towards there. She followed him down onto the ground level of the Castle and through different courtyards until they came up to a huge open field of manicured green grass surrounded by the outside ivy-covered stone wall of the castle.

As they stepped off the stone cobbled floor and onto

the field, Isa noticed the shooting ranges with targets and an assortment of dummies for sword practice. An array of weapons was laid out on racks throughout the edges of the field.

Turning to Benjamin patting him on the shoulder, she smiled as he looked at her surprised.

"Thank you, Benjamin, I think you just saved my life." She said jokingly.

⁓

Swinging one of the swords at her disposal, Isa let out her pent-up frustration. She needed to release her anger. As the sun had reached over the peaks of the hills, Isa knew that she had been there for at least a couple of hours but she didn't care. She needed to let out some energy, especially after the tea luncheon.

Off to the side watching Isa, Benjamin had placed himself down on the grass cross legged with his head in his palm. Having watched her for the past couple of hours, he couldn't leave Isa here by herself. He had promised Orion that he would look out for her.

Hearing the slow crunch of footsteps, he looked up

to see Orion standing next to him with his arms crossed watching Isa.

"What's up with her?" Orion asked as his brows furrowed still watching her. Benjamin shrugged going back to observing her.

"She asked to come here after the tea with your mother and the ladies of the court."

With Benjamin's comment, Orion hummed and approached Isa, unsheathing his own sword. Feeling a presence behind her, Isa swung her sword behind her as it clanged against Orion's own sword. Isa stared at him but her face seemed to relax, their swords still against each other.

"May I ask is something is bothering you?" Orion grinned. Isa nodded as she started lowering her sword from his and relaxing her grip, but Orion stopped her.

Smirking, Isa pulled back and lunged forward at him as Orion blocked her sword with ease. Now, instead of small whacks, clangs and clashes filled the clearing as they sparred against each other. Despite having already tired herself out, Orion was surprised that she was able to keep up with him.

"I rather not say," Isa swung her sword at him again. Another clang was heard as Orion blocked it and stepped forward to make his own offensive move, but Isa was too quick as she deflected it with ease.

"Is my mother to blame?" Orion said already a little out of breath. He would be really upset if it was his mother.

Isa shook her head landing another blow against his steel. Isa started deflecting his attacks with one hand easily like he was a student and she was the master. Orion breathed as he tried to gain the upper hand against Isa, but she was too quick. With another failed offensive move, Orion spoke again.

"Is the General to blame?" Orion continued.

Isa stopped pausing her attacks as she lowered her sword. Orion followed, worried. He watched her for some sort of emotion on her face. Orion found none but a blank expression as she kept her thoughts to herself.

"I'd rather finish what we started here," Isa said as she lifted her sword again twirling it her face changing quickly back to look at him.

She smirked as she stepped forward again towards Orion with her sword held high ready.

He went to deflect, but Isa stopped his sword with a powerful block, pushed it in a full circle and knocked it out of Orion's hand with so much force that he fell to the ground. Surprised, Orion blinked feeling the wind knocked out of him and found himself on the ground. Before he could regain his senses, Isa swiftly and quickly picked up his sword as she kneed him in the chest holding both of the swords above him ready in a striking position.

Seeing Isa on top of him, Orion laid still on the ground. He didn't move an inch as he regained his breath through his nose. Isa and Orion were silent as they stared at each other, their breathing tickling their faces. They were silent as they both kept staring at each other. Finally, after a second, Isa leaned in closer.

"I win," she whispered, smirking.

---

The hallway was dark, quiet and empty, the guards watched Isa intently as she passed them on her way towards Orion's room. Sighing, she lifted her hand to knock on Orion's door. Hesitating, Isa took a deep breath and knocked.

"Are you up, if you are not, I-," she whispered before his bedroom door swung open. "I can't sleep."

Orion looked at her softly before nodding.

He gestured for her to come inside as he moved over to let her in. Isa stepped into the room as Orion closed the door behind her with a soft thud. Looking around, Isa stood in the middle of his bedroom. The first thing she noticed was the maps of Atalia that hung above a dark wooden desk which was adorned with stacks of paper and books. A bookshelf stood next to the desk. Walking towards it, Isa read the book spines intrigued grazing a finger over the titles. Isa smiled to herself as she remembered when Orion had brought a book with him.

"Are you interested in a particular book?" Orion asked making Isa turn towards him. "These are just a collection of my favorite books from the Royal Library."

"The Royal Library?" Isa asked trying to suppress a yawn by covering her mouth with the back of her hand. Orion noticed and chuckled.

"Yes, there are so many. I will show tomorrow. You seem tired." He hovered a hand over her back to guide her as Isa turned towards Orion's bed.

"What's really bothering you tonight. Isa?"

Sighing sadly, Isa looked down.

Taking a deep breath, Orion looked at her before bringing her head into his chest. She could feel his heartbeat underneath her ear as Orion's hands threaded through her hair. Feeling him all around her, Isa closed her eyes as she melted into him.

"I'm worried about General Adrastus. He knows I'm here in the Castle." Isa said. "He used to be my mentor and now he turned evil. Like possessed. Back when I was in the special forces as you know, my team and I were assigned a mission which did not end go very well. We were captured by the enemy and imprisoned in Endrancia. But General Adrastus refused to send a rescue mission."

Orion open his mouth to speak but Isa continued.

"I heard from Lieutenant Carya that the General knew about our position in Endrancia and he made a pretty strong case to the King *against* bringing us back. Not worth saving us. Pawns in his war-game. He decided to abandon us. We were just another troop to him. My medal of honor was a threat to him and he found a way to get rid of me." Isa finished.

Orion remained speechless. He thought about what Ms. Whittle had told him. About Isa's bravery and how she deserved to be the General of Atalia's army. However being a commanding officer was a lifetime position. The only way to remove General Adrastus from his rank was if he was killed, or a challenge by combat.

"You are safe here. But did you notice the face the General gave when he saw you last night?" Orion said grinning.

Isa laughed.

Orion was learning more about her every day. She had suffered a lot and still helped Amarantha. Orion looked down at his hands as he rubbed his hands together thinking. *Would I be able to give her a new life? Would I be able to protect her? Even if I was next in line for the throne, would she be able to live in the Castle with me?*

After a moment of silence, Isa heard Orion speak.

"Stay," Orion whispered softly.

"What?" Isa asked confused as she turned to look at him.

"Stay longer in Deval," Orion said almost pleading.

*If I were to stay, I would need my allies in the Castle,*

she thought. Looking up, Isa turned to Orion who was waiting for her answer patiently his eyes watching her gently.

"Under one condition," Isa whispered smirking as she held up her pointer finger. Orion grinned chuckling before turning serious, coughing and nodding.

"Anything." He stated so softly and with such certainty that Isa paused for a second before speaking.

"I'd like Victoria and Laura to come and stay here with me."

# CHAPTER 13

Back in her everyday attire, her hair up in braids away from her face, Isa secured her daggers across her body. As she made her way through the castle, Isa found herself by the practice fields again. Isa shrugged contemplating. *Why not?*

Climbing down the stone steps, she walked into the clearing. Hearing a sigh and the release of a bowstring, she looked up to see Orion in the training field. Furrowing her eyebrows in confusion, she approached the training grounds crossing her arms as she watched him.

With his white shirt sleeves rolled up to his elbows, Orion held the bow he had originally brought with him the first time they met. Now, Isa could clearly see the details of the weapon. It was a beautifully crafted bow, with carvings of the faces of past Atalian kings. The bow string was white which was unusual, and Orion didn't have any arrows on him. It looked like he was just dry firing.

Stepping closer to him, Orion didn't acknowledge Isa's presence, but he knew she was there.

"You seem frustrated?" Isa asked as she stood by his side with her arms crossed. Orion didn't jump at her words, instead he sighed and lowered his bow.

"I don't seem to do anything right." Orion lifted the bow again. Staring at the target in front of him, he started dry firing again.

*He was a light sorcerer.* Isa remembered.

Even without hearing Orion's response, she was right. A light sorcerer had the ability to produce pure light energy arrows that never missed their target and defied all laws of nature. As Isa continued looking at Orion, she recalled what she learned many years ago about the first King of Atalia, Aila Dawn, Orion's ancestor. Aila Dawn was the founder of the Atalian Kingdom and the most powerful light sorcerer. Legend said that he was able to concentrate the energy of the sun in his hands.

"You can't produce the light arrows yet, can't you?" Isa asked inquisitively.

Sighing in defeat, Orion turned and walked towards the nearest bench sitting down with his head hung low. Isa followed as she sat down next to him. Orion rested the bow next to him gently as he grasped his hands on top of his lap.

"I should already be able to create a light arrow. But I don't understand what is happening to me." Orion shrugged looking around the empty training field as he rested his elbows on his legs.

"More practice?" Isa asked softly not intending it to sound rude. Orion sighed again as he looked at her, smiling softly.

"My father could do this magic when he turned twenty-two," Orion said, looking down at the bow, picking it up and placing it in his lap as he rubbed his thumb over the carvings.

"Light sorcery, or Lux Solis is one of the many magical abilities that is inherited. Essentially, it's passed down from father to son and it's something that all Atalian Kings had. That's why the Atalian flag has a white sun on it," Orion paused, sighing again turning towards Isa.

"I must be able to master my magic before I

am crowned as King, as my father, grandfather and great-grandfather did before me." Orion took a deep breath before placing the bow onto the bench next to him again. Hanging his head again, Isa waited silently as she let him process everything.

"The date is set for the coronation and my father is-," Orion said as he lifted his head again feeling better. Isa watched him, confused.

"My father will be holding a Ball at the winter solstice in preparation for my coronation when I turn twenty-five. Unlike the Kingdom of Endrancia or Zudora whose Kings should remain in the throne until their deaths, Atalian Kings reign until the next in line turns twenty-five years of age. The major lords and ladies from all over Atalia are coming to meet me," Orion stated as he started to play with his fingers before looking at Isa.

*He seems unsure. Hesitant. What is bothering him? He has to think about the future of his people.* Isa thought. *I am sitting next to the future King of Atalia after all.*

"I would like to have you with me, I mean go to the Ball with me."

Isa grinned at him as she laughed a little, turning towards him.

"Are you asking *me* to the Ball?" Isa smirked, readjusting her seat with her hands. Orion immediately turned away embarrassed, placing a hand on his neck.

"I know it has been very frustrating for you being at the castle and I understand if -." Isa held a hand to stop Orion. He closed his mouth nervously and watched her silent.

"Orion, I don't know what to say. I-, I came here to have an audience with your father and to plead for help for my village. " She hesitated placing a hand on his shoulder.

"I sent an invitation to your friends Victoria and Laura this morning while you were sleeping," Orion answered truthfully. "You need to stay. I would be honored to have you by my side."

Isa looked up into his eyes.

"Really? If that is what you want, your Majesty. I will stay."

Orion grinned at her as she smiled back hiding the expression of her doubtful eyes .

# CHAPTER 14

The first flurries of winter had started to sprout up as the weather cooled down. The King decided that the ball would be held during the winter solstice to celebrate the upcoming year.

It had been two weeks since Orion had asked Isa to take her to the ball and his mother had invited Isa to attend numerous private sessions with her. Trying not to seem bored, Isa nodded leaning against her chair as Orion's mother kept talking about the history of the Kingdom. It felt more of schooling session than regular luncheons, which made Isa feel a bit suspicious about the Queen's intentions. The Queen was teaching her all sorts of topics: The battles of Atalia, the names of the Lords and Ladies of Atalia, their Allies, Atalian exports and imports, and most of all, proper royal etiquette.

Isa was happy when her friends Victoria and Laura had

arrived in Deval shortly after Orion sent them the invitation. Hugging them both tightly, Isa had allies she could trust in the castle. She knew they would keep an eye on her when Orion or Benjamin weren't there. They kept Isa company and supported her during the tea luncheons Isa has to attend with the Queen. Laura and Victoria seemed to really enjoy themselves. They blended in perfectly well talking with the ladies of the court and standing their grounds.

During one of the Queen's lectures, Isa stared at her etiquette book as the Queen demonstrated them in action. Isa had been reading for hours had the sun now had moved to the other side of the castle. Playing with a little piece of loose string on her shirt sleeve, Isa was quiet barely listening as Orion's mothers voice drowned out. Isa thought, *why do I need to be here? Why do I have to learn all these things? I came here to save my village.*

Orion's mother's voice continued on.

Isa made eye contact with the Queen nodding her head to seem like she was invested in her lesson, but once her eyes left Isa's face, she went right back into picking at the thread.

Suddenly, she popped her head up, eyes wide, Isa needed to leave the room and escape these lessons.

Raising a hand to stop Orion's mother, Isa spoke silencing the Queen.

"Will you excuse me?" Isa said placing her napkin on the table standing up.

"My dear, are you unwell?" Orion's mother asked as Isa nodded leaving the Queen's private room.

After, Isa closed the door behind her, the Queen smiled cunningly.

———◦———

Isa released a deep breath and took off. Running through the halls of the castles, she dodged past servants as she searched for Victoria and Laura. She needed the only people she trusted the most. Turning another corner, Isa finally found Victoria flirting with one of the guards. Rolling her eyes, Isa came up from behind Victoria and looped her arm around hers.

"I need you and Laura, now," Isa whispered into Victoria's ear. Understanding, Victoria said her last words to the guard before Isa walked off with her in tow.

"What's all this fuss?" Victoria huffed jokingly as Isa lead her through the castle.

Finally, Isa and Victoria found Laura talking to Benjamin. Benjamin said something as Laura laughed along. Apologizing to Benjamin, Isa dragged the two of them into the royal library.

Letting go of their arms, Isa turned to them both.

"You know the private lessons I've been having with Orion's mother, right?"

Victoria and Laura looked at each other confused and nodded as they watched Isa's chest fall up and down to her beathing.

"What about them?" Victoria asked crossing her arms.

"Well, I don't think I am fit for this lifestyle. And I just realized why I've been going to these lessons," Isa said trying to see their reaction, but they didn't seem surprised.

"Isa, you need to figure this out," Victoria answered sarcastically. "I mean you and Orion are..." Victoria laughed seeing Isa's face.

"No, I-I can't." Isa said taking a step back doubting herself. Laura shook her head at Victoria's comment, and instead took the lead.

"Look Isa, I believe that the Queen is preparing you for the life of a royal. You should think over this and decide if this is what you want. To be honest, you need to talk to Orion. You could be the next ruler our kingdom needs," Laura finished smiling softly at her.

Isa took a breath calming her fast heartbeat. Isa pulled both Victoria and Laura into a hug.

⬦

Meanwhile Orion headed straight to the throne room determined. When he entered, General Adrastus stared intensely at Orion as he started leaving the room. Orion did the same and thought, *if only my eyes could have the power to kill.*

"Father, may I speak with you privately?" Orion said as his father waved off his advisors.

Stepping up on the dais and sitting down on his throne tired, the King waved his son over concerned. "What is on your mind, son? Is it about the Ball?"

Orion took a deep breath lifting his hand making eye contact with his father. "I want you to know that I am planning to propose to Isa at the Ball," Orion said determined, but worried about his reaction.

The King had anticipated this conversation with Orion.

"What are you going to do about the Endrancian's and our treaty ?" Orion's father asked watching, testing Orion. His son took a deep breath interlocking his hands behind his back before answering.

"Amarantha's parents responded to my new proposal to continue with the treaty terms except for the marriage since Amarantha is already married."

"And how did they respond?" The King asked raising an eyebrow intrigued.

"They weren't completely happy receiving the news that their daughter was married to a commoner but I managed to convince them since Amarantha is married to an Atalian afterall."

The King didn't say anything.

"I would ask Isa before the ball, but I believe our people will love Isa. She is iswell respected and admired-," he started before his father lifted a hand to stop him. Orion stopped talking as he gulped worried his father would disagree.

"Is this what you really want? Do you think Isa would be right of our kingdom?" The King asked his son. Orion took a deep breath closing his eyes before opening them to answer.

"I want her by my side."

"You need to think carefully and not only with your heart. Do you have strong feeling towards her?" The King asked gently.

Orion grinned before looking straight at his father composing himself.

"I do. I ..." Orion paused. "I want to propose to Isa where you proposed to mother."

The King was silent before stepping down from the dais.

"You ready, my son," Orion's father said as he embraced Orion.

"There is still one problem. I can't use the bow yet- I can't create light," he started, but was interrupted by his father. Releasing himself from Orion, the King grabbed both of Orion's shoulders.

"It will come with time. A catalyst is the key. Light sorcery is not like other magical powers in this world.

It determines whether you are ready to wield it or not. When Alia Dawn declared independence from Zudora, that was his catalyst."

With that the King pulled Orion into his embrace once again.

"What matters is that you faced the Endrancian's diplomatically and thought about the kingdom. After all of my years as King, I have found that kindness and compassion are the best qualities a leader can have. If you do not realize that you will never be respected as a future monarch." Coming out of the embrace, the King continued.

"My father before me was not as such and your mother showed me that I can break that chain. Saying this, the way you held yourself and placed the Atalian people before your own today proves that. It proves that you value your future position as King, and I couldn't have been prouder to have you as a son. A true King shows love and empathy not only to his future kingdom but to his future Queen. I think she'll make a lovely monarch," the King pulled Orion back into his grasp giving him one last hug.

Strolling through the castle, Orion heard Isa's voice as he stopped to look down at the training grounds. Intrigued, Orion walked over to the balcony leaning against the railing on the second story. He noticed Isa and Benjamin standing side by side each with wooden swords in their hands. Mesmerized, he watched as Isa slowly swung the sword in the air talking to Benjamin, guiding him.

Doing the last technique, Isa stood up fully and lifted a hand to high five Benjamin. Looking proud at himself, he high fived her back. Orion chuckled to himself on top of the railing. Isa lifted her head and finally noticed him. Seeing him standing there, Isa smiled wide.

Then Orion heard laughter from someone else. He looked over to the side and saw Laura reading a book laughing at Isa and Benjamin. Having heard Laura's laughter, Benjamin stuck a tongue out at her.

Hearing soft footsteps, Orion turned to the side and saw his mother walking towards him. Placing a comforting hand around his shoulders, she gently rubbed his back.

"I knew I would find you here," she said turning to see Orion's gaze on Isa and Benjamin. Orion didn't say anything as he watched them practice. She noticed where he was looking as she smiled at him.

"I am not sure if she is ready, Orion. However, I am here to support your decision and your father's decision. Did you speak with him? " His mother asked and this time he did answer.

"Yes," he nodded.

"And?"

"He accepted my decision," Orion said smiling happily as he looked at his mother before turning around again towards the training grounds.

His mother watched him, softening her gaze.

"How is Isa doing with your lessons?" Orion didn't think these lessons were needed, but his mother had insisted.

"I think she is doubting herself."

As Orion watched Isa train with Benjamin, he wanted to make sure that Isa was ready to be by his side.

"Have you talked with her about your intentions yet?" His mother asked Orion.

He was silent, his chest fluttering in doubt.

# CHAPTER 15

Isa could not stop thinking about her conversation with Victoria and Laura. The Queen had really overwhelmed her with lessons after lessons, the lingering headache growing. *But if I were to become Queen, I'd want to rule side by side with Orion. Change the Kingdom for the better. I want to make sure every village in the Kingdom has enough provisions and resources. I don't want to be reduced to mainly having a title. I would like to do more,* she thought.

The sound of a door opening and closing caused Isa to come out of her thoughts. Orion never left his room this late at night. Gently stepping into the hallway, Isa used her door to shield her body as she noticed Orion's figure, The guards were still posted at her door. She sighed.

Surprised, Orion turned around seeing her and then smiled walking back towards her.

"My father has requested my presence in the throne room. I won't be long." Orion said as he searched her eyes and moved a fallen stray piece of hair away from her face.

Isa nodded before stepping back into her room and closing the door behind her. Jumping into the bed, Isa grabbed the covers over herself trying to close her eyes.

She didn't know how long she had been sleeping for when the sound of the window creaking open made her become alert. Isa thought she left the window open. However, she could hear footsteps getting closer to her bed.

Trying to stay still she tried to distinguish in the dark who was in her room from her peripherals but she couldn't see anything. Calming her breathing, she tried to find her weapons but they were too far away from her.

*Shit.*

Feeling the weight of the bed dip behind her, Isa stayed still. If she stayed silent, she could gain the upper hand. *Never let them predict your next move.* Hearing the unsheathing of a weapon, Isa immediately turned onto her back, hands flying up to her face as she caught the dagger inches from her neck.

Grabbing the blade with her bare hands, blood dripped down the steel, coating her neck and nightgown in red. Isa pushed the dagger away from her body with such a force that the dark figure fell down to the ground dropping the dagger.

"Who are you? Who sent you?" Isa demanded lifting the dagger from the floor and pointing it to the intruder.

Swinging a fist at her, Isa dodged it and used her own weight to twist around to headlock the intruder.

"Fine, we'll do it the hard way," Isa winced.

Isa knocked them down to the ground. They were holding their head squirming on the floor. Frustrated and tired, Isa walked to her desk to grab her staff looping it over her shoulder.

Their body lay unmoving on the floor as Isa sighed in tiredness. Grabbing their arms, Isa ignored the pain coming from her bloody hands as she dragged the body to her door. Pushing the door open with her body, she managed to pull them out as the guards at her door looked at her in shock.

"I need your help to take them to the throne room."

The throne room had a large table in the middle with

a map of Atalia that the King, Orion, General Adrastus, and advisors were pondering over as Isa and the guards walked in unannounced with the unconscious body.

Seeing Isa first, the King and Orion immediately stood up in shock.

"What is the meaning of this?" He asked as the guards continued dragging the body further into the throne room.

Orion noticed Isa and his eyes widened.

"Isa? Your bleeding!" Orion said as he ran over to her. He gasped in worry seeing her hands. He ripped a part of his shirt and wrapped pieces of cloth around her hands.

Tired and leaning into Orion, Isa watched as the guards searched the body. She finally spoke.

"They tried to kill me."

Pulling the mask off, everyone could see a young man with a huge bleeding wound on his head. Isa came closer to the body and she inspected the black uniform. Kneeling with Isa, Orion saw the Endrancian symbol on them. His eyes widened. *That couldn't be possible.*

"Guards, take him away into the dungeons!" The King commanded.

"I want a full investigation done, General," Orion commanded as General Adrastus nodded slowly.

"I will look into it, my Prince." And with that the General left the room with the unconscious bodies.

"He won't do it, Isa whispered to herself as she looked down the pool of blood that had been left on the stone floor.

With an arm over her shoulders, Orion led Isa back to his bedroom never once letting her go. The guards posted there immediately opened Orion's door as he hurried in with Isa. Setting her down on his bed, he cupped her face checking her eyes but she looked down at her hands. Orion grabbed and kissed her hands.

Tears started flowing down her face. *Someone had tried to kill me. I haven't felt this fear since I was in the special forces. I had let my guard down. I should never have come to Deval.*

Tightening his grip on her, Orion said, "I promised to protect you."

"I know the General planned this attack." Isa started to panic as Orion pulled her in closer.

"We shouldn't jump to conclusions until we finish doing a full investigation," Orion reassured her but he had a feeling she was right.

Orion wiped her tears away from her cheeks with his hand and continued.

"You have my full support to catch the person responsible who planned this assault on you," Orion said, staring straight into Isa's eyes.

"Let's get this son of a bitch," Isa whispered, determined.

⸻ ✦ ⸻

Isa didn't want to be alone.

It was hard to fall asleep. Letting out a breath of frustration, Isa turned over onto her other side to see Orion resting next to her. At peace with his eyes closed, his face was relaxed but she could tell he was somewhat awake

"Orion?" She whispered. Opening his eyes, he slowly readjusted himself to turn towards Isa grabbing her outstretched hand. She accepted curling her hand into his.

"You can't sleep?" He whispered in response.

Isa nodded her head as she curled deeper into the covers bringing them up to her chin without releasing their grasped hands.

"Come here," Orion whispered, letting go of her hand as he reached out and wrapped an arm underneath the bedcover pulling her into his chest. A little surprised, Isa smiled and sighed into him hearing his heartbeat as he placed a hand over her head. Feeling warm and secure, she clung onto Orion's nightshirt pressing her face into him. He stroked her hair as she stayed silent enjoying his comforting touch.

"In the morning, I'll have more guards posted out-side-," he started but Isa interrupted him.

"No," she said placing her hand on his chest to stop him talking. "I don't want anyone to know about this assassination attempt on me. It can cause the villages to revolt."

"Then I want someone with you at all times," Orion said as he sat up as well next to her putting a gentle hand on her back.

"Orion, I was a soldier. I can protect myself. I was able to defend myself." Isa added, smirking a little.

" It's just...,You could have died tonight." Orion paused, trying not to raise his voice as he rubbed his face.

Glancing at his eyes briefly, Isa couldn't help but immediately look down. His blue eyes were filled with such tenderness she knew that he was only trying to protect her as he promised he would.

"I don't want to lose you," Orion whispered gently as his eyes fluttered, staring into her own. Seeing this Isa sighed sadly.

"You won't." She softly grasped his wrist moving her thumb over his hand.

He gazed at her, enchanted

An eternity seemed to pass as they both stared into each other's eyes. As Orion softly caressed her face, Isa's couldn't help the blood that rushed to her cheeks. Orion searched her face as his focus drifted down then back to her eyes

Slowly, Isa saw Orion lean in closer tilting his head. She did the same and went up to meet him. Feeling his lips pressed up against hers, Isa closed her eyes accepting it. Heart skipping a beat, Isa lifted her own hands to cup Orion's face to bring him in closer to her deepening their kiss.

Then Orion pulled back slightly as their noses still

touched. They shared the same breath before he whispered.

"Tell me if you want me to stop," Orion breathed against her lips resting his forehead against hers as Isa's heart fluttered sending a shiver down her spine.

"Never."

Reaching back to kiss her, Orion wrapped an arm around Isa's back pushing her body almost bringing her into his lap. He kissed her gently and carefully, like she was going to break if he went too far, but she could feel the tension and deepness from their intimacy. Their lips molded together perfectly. Releasing him, Isa opened her eyes again and looked back up at Orion softly.

And that's when she knew she had finally made her decision.

"Will you accept me as your suitor and stay in Deval with me?" Orion whispered, searching her eyes for any sort of doubt.

"Yes," Isa said as Orion chuckled the start of tears in his eyes from happiness.

The long kiss turned into quick pecks as Orion leaned back and gazed at Isa, smoothing her hair away from her face. Inspecting her face, he smiled gently at her. Sighing happily, Orion grinned as they both slowly laid back down on the bed not once breaking eye contact.

Relishing the feeling of being this close with Orion continued to fuel something stronger within Isa.

Isa was more than ever determined to catch the person who had sent the assassin to kill her. She wants more than ever to live a life freely and happily with Orion in Deval. She wanted to be free from the torment of always having to look over her shoulder every time she was in the castle grounds.

# CHAPTER 16

The early morning light woke Isa up as it streamed right onto her face from the glass window. She opened her eyes and was met with Orion's white shirt. Lifting her head slightly, Isa realized that she had slept on his chest as one of his arms was still wrapped around her protectively. Isa gazed at him noticing his mouth was slightly open. Remembering what had happened last night, Isa turned away from him and pressed her face into her pillow.

Feeling Isa's weight off him, Orion blinked awake making sure she was alright. Looking around he saw Isa turned away from him.

"Morning," Orion stated tiredly as he kept Isa in front of him.

"Good morning to you too, sleepy head," Isa whispered as Orion smiled at her.

"How are you feeling?" Orion whispered.

Seeing where his gaze landed, Isa frowned as she looked down at her hands.

"Better now," Isa smiled and looked at Orion.

Isa stayed wrapped in Orion's warmth as she played with his hands intertwining their fingers and tracing shapes into his palm. Sighing, she closed her eyes in peace until her hands started tingling.

Isa knew what it needed to be done.

Turning around to face him, Isa smiled sadly and nodded. She knew that staying in the castle with Orion would come with a price. She needed to be *The Phantom* again. The soldier that had mercilessly killed many people, the ghost of her past. *That's the only way.*

Orion could sense her tension and frustration. He calmed her down as Isa nodded. With an arm around her lower back, Orion walked Isa back to her bedroom. Opening her door, Orion led her inside as Isa stepped in. Examining the chaos and mess of the room after the attack, Isa moved the curtains of her window to bring in the morning breeze as she finally noticed the dark dried blood puddle on her bed.

She averted her eyes and slowly turned her head towards Orion. Seeing this, he reached a hand to her cheek moving her head to look at him again.

"Let's go and find out who they are and bring them to justice."

Heading down to the dungeons of the castle with Orion, Isa held the assassin's dagger that she had wrapped in her dirty nightgown. The guards and prison keeper let them walk through the dungeons. Shivering a bit, Isa remembered when she was in there not long ago.

Unlocking the door, the prison keeper pushed the solid door open as they walked into a cold drafty stone room that belonged to the person who had tried to kill her. He was sitting in a chair behind a table tied up as guards were posted around him. His head injury had stopped bleeding as Isa raised her eyebrows. Watching Isa stride up to the table in front of the man, Orion directed the guards out of the room and closed the door behind them.

"Do you know why I'm here?" Isa started by looking up at the man tied up in front of her. Orion noticed that her eyes were emotionless, cold, calculating. This was the Phantom he was watching now.

The assassin in the chair nodded scoffing, not looking at Isa.

"Who sent you? Why did you try to kill me?" Isa asked. He looked older than her with pale skin and straight black hair that was matted with dried blood. The man was quiet, not saying anything to her. He scoffed at her again looking away smirking, his leg tapping away.

He remained silent while he started licking his dried and cracked lips.

Like lightning, Isa reached over grabbing a fistful of his hair and slammed his face onto the table. Hearing a crack, Orion flinched a little.

"The Endrancian Royals sent me," he said as blood dripped down his nose.

Isa stepped closer to the prisoner determined to throw a punch this time.

" Wait, wait...! The deal between Atalia and Endrancia was supposed to include an arranged marriage with the Prince. But the Princess escaped and is in hiding married to another Atalian."

"How does he know that? No one is supposed to know about this except for my father," Orion whispered behind them in shock.

Isa turned back to the prisoner.

"You wear Endrancian uniforms, but you carry an Atalian blade." Isa reached over and unraveled the dagger before slamming it into the table making it stick into the wooden table. The man stared at it shocked.

He sighed as he turned away from her.

"Tell me, where are you from?" She asked again.

"Endrancia."

Isa rubbed her face in frustration.

"You don't even look Endrancian. You don't even have their culture markings either," Isa said, pausing as she leaned in closer.

Stepping around the table and towards the prisoner, she turned his chair around to face him with one hand. Suddenly, he seemed to know what she was about to do.

"Oh no," he gulped.

Staring at the man, Isa placed one of her bandaged hands to his forehead. With her hand grasping his head, she looked down straight into his eyes. "With this hand you shall tell the truth," Isa recited, spreading her fingers over his forehead.

After her words, the assassin locked onto Isa's eyes in a trance like he was hypnotized.

"Let's try this again. Tell me who sent you?" Isa said calmly but still demanding. Waiting a second, the man didn't say anything, until Isa pressed her hand harder into his forehead.

"I was hired; I currently serve the General for the Atalian armies. I was given a mission," he said in a monotone voice.

Sighing, Isa released his forehead. He dropped his head down onto his chest panting as he regained himself coming out of her spell. Looking down at her hands, Isa thought that the bandages were preventing her from using the magic she possessed. Curling her fingers into a fist, she sighed in defeat as she started walking away from the man.

"I know of you. *The Phantom.* You saved a lot of people in Endrancia."

Isa turned around sharply watching him look up at her slowly blinking.

"What did you say?" She asked cautiously.

"My brother, Samuel Huegen. He served with you; you saved him."

Isa's eyes widened. Seeing her shocked face, he chuckled regaining his breath and licked his chapped lips before speaking to her again.

"The person who sent me was General Adrastus," the man said softly in-between breaths.

Coming out of her surprise, she knew that this man had risked his life by telling her who was behind her assassination attempt. This soldier was another pawn used by General Adrastus just like she had been.

"I'm going to kill him," Isa whispered, staring at the solid door.

"Wait, Isa. What are you planning to do?" He asked, grabbing her arm and making her stop before opening the door.

Isa didn't look at Orion.

"He does not deserve my mercy, Orion."

And with that, he released her arm.

Isa had been silent ever since they had come from the dungeons. As they reached their rooms, Isa stopped in front of hers. Noticing she wasn't following him anymore, Orion looked behind him worried. Isa hesitated before speaking.

"I'd like to be alone in my own room. I need some time to think and put this whole mess behind me and rest. For now, I won't be attending your mother's lessons." Isa rambled on looking down at the ground. Orion turned towards her smiling gently and walked up to her. Gently lifting her chin with his hand, he responded as she went silent looking up at him.

"I understand. I will let my mother know."

Locking the door behind her, she waited for complete silence. Isa pressed her hands against her cheeks trying to cool her face down before immediately heading to the window. She stepped onto her balcony and looked up at the full bright moon before bringing her gaze down to the ever-expansive forest. Isa watched for a second as the slight breeze in the air rustled the dark leaves of the forest. As the wind cooled her face, she took a deep breath to calm her beating heart before proceeding with her plan.

Pushing her lips together, she let out a long and powerful whistle. The sound disappeared into the night as she waited. Suddenly, Isa could pick up the flapping of wings. It intensified as a small black winged body flew out from within the forest and towards her. Reaching a hand out for him, Isa watched as Ayden flew over and perched himself in front of Isa on her forearm.

"Ayden, wonderful to see you." she said, smiling as Ayden nodded.

"*Isa, how can I help you?*" Ayden asked as Isa sighed.

She explained everything to Ayden. What had happened to her in the castle, the attempt against her life, her frustrations and the truth about the General.

"*It's not fair what you had to go through. How can I be of service to you?*"

"I need you to do something for me," Isa asked.

"*Whatever you need, Isa,*" Ayden stated as he rustled his feathers. Isa grinned at Ayden stroking the top of his head.

"Gather as many of your friends as you can and I need you to be my eyes and ears to spy on someone for me. I want you to be his shadow," Isa said seriously.

"*Who?*" The falcon titled his head up at her.

"An old General of mine."

# CHAPTER 17

A couple of days later, Edvard, the raven had perched on Isa's balcony railing with some news from Ayden. The raven shared with her that the General had left the castle a few days ago and was heading to the Eastern border of Atalia. *The General was NOT in the capital? Why did the King send him away? Was Orion aware of his father's new orders?*

After the raven left, Isa started walking to the training ground. She needed to think and clear her mind. She needed to be focused and keep practicing and be ready.

The castle was quiet at dawn. Not a single word was heard on the hallways. As the sun started raising, she could hear some servants doing their early morning chores, but no one bothered Isa in the training grounds as she kept focusing her energy on the dummy. A layer of sweat covered her exposed skin as Isa took a breather letting her sword hang down by her side.

Hearing the crunch of footsteps behind her, Isa knew Orion was near.

Isa stopped sighing as she wiped the sweat off her forehead.

"It seems you've been here for a while. What is bothering you?" Orion said.

Isa looked down at her feet, guilty. Kicking the dummy one last time for good measure, she sighed before talking.

"Something doesn't feel right, Orion. What the prisoner told me doesn't make sense. Why would the General order an Atalian soldier to kill me? And blame it on Endrancia? You talked to Amarantha's parents, and convinced them about her daughter's decision to marry Quinn, right?" Isa said finally turning towards Orion who was standing there with his arms crossed frowning.

"Yes, of course I did," He asked tilting his head to the side.

"It seems that the General was trying to gain my attention," Isa paused whispering, "to distract me from something more important."

Isa looked down at the ground pacing having abandoned her training. Thinking, she rubbed her hand over her face.

"Look, I never told the General about the Endrancian new treaty," Orion said.

"He must have someone else spying or he intercepted the message," Isa whispered as Orion followed her confused. Isa stopped pacing and spoke to Orion directly.

"You know the General is not in Deval and he is heading to the border near Zudora?" Isa told Orion.

"I did not know. I don't recall my father ever sending him away," Orion said shrugging his shoulders.

Isa slowly grinned at him. *What was the General up to?*

"I'm not sure why. Zudora is dealing with their own political civil war there right now," Isa pointed a finger at him thinking.

Orion shook his head waving his hands in front of him.

"Wait, wait. How do you know the General is there?" He asked stepping closer to her. Isa chuckled awkwardly looking away from him, guilty as she inspected her sword again.

"A little friend told me. I have eyes and ears in the forest."

Sighing, Orion thought of Ayden. But Isa continued.

"Orion, why would the General want to send an assassin after me? He obviously didn't want the new treaty to happen and he wanted to scare me off and force me to leave Deval in fear and to never come back," Isa finished as she turned back to the training dummy again.

Orion remained silent and started thinking about what Ms. Whittle had told him about the General and how he has treated Isa. The General didn't want Isa in a higher position over himself so he wanted Isa out of the picture all together. Either for Isa to run back to Liliane in fear or better yet, to die.

*I won't let that happen.*

⊷◆⊶

Isa continued training every day. She felt stronger and ready to confront the General upon his return. It was a dark and rainy day when Victoria burst into Isa's room. She was sitting with one of the books from the library when she looked up at her blonde-haired friend confused. Breathing heavily, Victoria was trying so hard to talk.

"What is it, Victoria?" Isa said standing up placing her

book on her desk before stepping towards Victoria. Taking a deep breath, Victoria finally looked up at her. "The General is back."

Isa didn't even let Victoria finish before she immediately walked out of her room. Striding into the hallway, Victoria tried to stop her.

"Isa! Be careful. You can't just do this!" Victoria yelled from behind her. Victoria desperately tried to slow her down, but she kept shrugging her off. Determined, Isa pushed the doors open bursting through the throne room. Her eyes scanning the room looking for the General.

Furious, Isa locked eyes with the General who stood next to the King as if he was expecting her arrival.

Seeing Isa, Orion immediately jumped in front of her holding his hands out in front of him.

"Isa-," he started as she come up to him.

"Don't try and stop me, Orion."

Orion stood still in front of her as time seemed to slow down. Isa stepped past him pulling his sword from around his waist. Orion watched her unsheathe his own sword from his belt. With a weapon gripped tightly in her hold, Isa charged at her former General. Screaming, she swung her sword at him as he pulled out his own. Their swords met with a clash that rang throughout the throne room.

"I challenge you to a duel by combat, traitor!" Isa screamed.

The King seemed to be confused having stepped back away from them.

"I demand an explanation. What is the matter here?" His voice echoing across the throne room while staring at Isa and the General for answers.

"This soldier is overreacting, your Majesty." General Adrastus strongly announced.

"Overreacting?!" Isa yelled as Orion stopped her before she could strike back with her sword. Wrapping his arms around her waist, he pulled her away.

"You sent another soldier to kill me! It was you!" Isa screamed against Orion's arms.

The King turned to Isa first his face crunched in concentration. "Isa, compose yourself," he said before turning to General Adrastus shocked at this new information.

"General, care to explain, Is this true?"

"Father, it's true. Isa and I have the prisoner's testimony to prove it," Orion said feeling Isa relax against him. He released his grasp on her as guards started surrounding them.

"General, any words?" The King said watching the General as he stayed silent accepting his fate. The King sighed and waved the guards over.

"Isa, your challenge has been accepted. Guards, prepare for a trial by combat. Take them to the stone corral," the King said as Isa bowed her head at him as the guards grabbed the Generals' arms leading him out of the throne room. Isa followed them with a frown still gripping Orion's sword tightly in her hand.

"Wait! Hold on, father you cannot allow this combat!" Orion said walking up to his father, but the King held a hand to stop him.

"Father, listen. He'll use this opportunity to kill her!" Orion yelled worried as he tried to think of another way. *Was his father in favor of letting* this comba*t proceed? Why?*

The King sighed putting a hand of his son's shoulder hoping to calm Orion down.

"Orion, listen to me. If she wins she will replace the General. It's a matter of honor. This is Isa's personal battle."

———◆———

The clouds had cleared Isa stood on the sandy gravel of the stone corral with Orion's sword gripped tightly in her hands. She had followed the guards as they led her and the General to the grounds outside of the castle. General Adrastus was on his knees making sure he had his own sword with him. As Isa stood before the General, she became the Phantom.

Following the rules for trail by combat, each fighter had a weapon. They could kill each other, but no use of magic was permitted.

As the King, his advisors, and Orion came closer to the corral, Isa waited until they were all seated before turning to face her former commander.

"Explain yourself, General Adrastus! Any last words?" Isa asked as she walked up to him. Once she was directly in front of him, he slowly lifted his head to smirk up at her.

"You were in my way," he stated like it was obvious.

"How was I in your way? I respected you! You were my commander. I followed your orders. You trained me for the special forces!" She stated desperately. He was silent, not even a hint of empathy in his eyes.

"I would find out sooner or later? I had allies," Isa added.

"I had a mission to fulfill," he said as Isa turned towards him. On guard, ready to fight.

"Who sent you in this mission? She asked waiting for his answer.

"You will never know."

Suddenly with a yell, the General jumped up onto his feet and swung his sword at her. Barely missing, Isa stepped back in shock. Standing and finally facing each other, Isa stared into the General's dark black eyes as her heart drummed against her ribcage.

"While I was away, Princess. I discovered who you really are. I know you better than you do," he said looking down at his hands, clenching them into fists.

Shocked, Isa's heart kept drumming away as she tried to keep her breathing to a normal pace. Standing her ground, Isa stared at the General Adrastus. *He called me "Princess".*

Suddenly, the General's sword evaporated into thin air as his hands started glowing and developing a dark black and purple aura.

*No magic. No magic during this combat.*

"General Adrastus! No magic!" The King yelled standing up from the stands.

Lifting his hands into the sky and screaming, black and translucent horrific shadowy figures shot from his hands surrounding the edges of the stone corral and filling the whole amphitheater.

A shiver ran down Isa's spine.

"You wanted a trial by combat, so be it. I don't usually kill royalty, but I will do an exception with you," he said as he pushed a hand towards her.

Barely dodging a huge wave of shadows, Isa rolled out of the way.

Standing up, Isa tightened her grip on Orion's sword and frowned, concentrating. She could feel the dark power pulsing from him, but what kind of magic was this? Now with both hands on the sword, she let out a battle cry as she ran towards. Dodging the shadows, she managed to swing at him, but he was too quick. He was not fighting to his full potential.

Landing onto the ground with an umph, her body rolled across the sand until she hit the stone edge. Gasping for air, Isa stood up as her arms shook beneath her. Lifting her head, she saw the small figure of her former commander in the distance. Trying to control her breathing, she stayed on the ground trying to assess her situation.

Isa needed to change her tactics.

Seeing Orion's sword laying against the sand near her, Isa crawled towards the weapon before grasping it and lifting herself off of the ground.

Smirking, General Adrastus released another wave of shadows at her. Preparing for the impact, she crossed her arms in front of her as she dug her heels into the ground. An immense pressure pushed against her arms as Isa gritted her teeth, her feet slowly sliding against the gravel. Laughing in the distance made her look up from her hands gritting her teeth as some blood seeped from in between them. The General had brought back the shadows to him, so he could recharge for his next attack.

"You are useless, Princess!"

Spitting onto the ground, Isa watched as the shadow's waved behind him in a collective. So that's what this was then, shadow magic. Isa watched the red liquid drip from her palms and onto the sand in front of her like water droplets. Mesmerized, her chest moved up and down rapidly, she watched the blood like river trail down her palm.

Like a spark, the same feeling she had experienced while in Endrancia returned. The same blind hatred mixed with rage and power shivered throughout her body. Letting out a gasp, images of Najia's dead body burned behind her eyes. Shaking her head, Isa closed her eyes trying to get these images out of her mind as more of the dark red blood dripped down onto the sandy gravel beneath her.

Opening her eyes, Isa took a deep breath through her nose as she gained the strength to lift her head. General Adrastus was a small speck within an aura of purple as Isa stared at him. Standing before him sharp and focused made him raise an eyebrow as he prepared for another attack.

Breathing through her nose, Isa trusted her body as

she rubbed her hands together covering them in her own blood. Seeing Orion's sword still sticking out of the ground, she stepped towards it her feet dragging behind her. Gripping the sword out of the sandy gravel, the hilt stained red from her bloody hands.

Sprinting through the parting of the shadows, she held up her hand when she needed too as the shadows hissed at her blood covered hand. Distracted by the shadows, General Adrastus appeared from within the barrier of purple and black with his arms out to the sides his palms up shadows still manifesting from them.

Seeing another clearing, Isa managed to swing her weapon at him. As more shadows burst from his palms, she hoped this work.

"This is for all those you have hurt," Isa whispered as she gritted her teeth. Only just realizing her attack, the General's eyes widened as she sliced into his torso with a yell.

Isa's voice echoed through the amphitheater as silence followed.

With the sword still lodged in his torso, General Adrastus dropped to his knees slowly pulling Orion's sword out. It fell to the ground with a clang as black blood seeped from in-between his hands. Standing in front of him, Isa froze watching the blood spill to the ground in heaps.

Screaming in torture, his body convulsed as his eyes started bleeding. The black blood flowed down his skin as he tried to claw at his eyes leaving red gashes across his face.

Isa watched as the shadows started appearing again. Watched as they seemed to be traveling through his body, eating him from the inside before tearing their way through. The shadows turned against him as they encompassed him.

The General's body still crumbling to the ground, his body shaking horrifically. Looking up with bloody eyes at Isa one last time, he whispered to her.

"You are a threat to us all, Princess Isa Bertocchi."

With those last words, the General's body ceased movement

Isa froze, eyes wide open. *He called me Princess Isa Bertocchi.*

Feeling liberated, Isa's body shook in tears as she

dropped down onto all fours. Breathing hard, Isa heard Orion's voice and saw his running figure come closer to her. Feeling her knees on the sandy gravel, she watched the ground with blurry eyes from tears and bits of blood as she collapsed losing consciousness.

———◦———

Gasping for air, Isa wake up in her bed panicking.

*The battle with her old General. He had died right in front of her revealing her true name. She was a Princess. Did that really happen? Was it all a dream or was it real?*

"Hey, hey, hey, Isa, I'm here." Orion whispered sitting next to her. Turning towards him, she leaped into his arms grasping onto him with a cry. He immediately wrapped his arms around her, pulling her close to him.

"I'm so glad you're alive," Orion whispered as Isa buried her face into his chest as she started sobbing. Shushing her, he cuddled her as he rocked them both together slowly. Silent, Orion kept Isa close to him letting her release all her tension from the battle.

"He's gone. He is dead," Orion answered.

Isa nodded her head into his chest.

"It wasn't a dream then?" She whispered.

"No, it wasn't a dream. You defeated him. I am so proud of you," Orion said cupping her face. Isa smiled at him.

"How long have I been out for?" Isa asked looking around her bedroom before turning towards the morning sun.

"A couple of days. You lost a lot of blood, and it seemed your body just needed to time to rest." Orion smiled at her as she did the same.

Looking down at her clean and bandaged hands, she could feel the ache of her wounds all over her body. Remembering the battle, Isa was trying to recall the General's last words. Isa chose not to say anything to Orion.

Orion continued lifting her chin.

"You're the new General now. You defeated him and you have become rightfully the General of the Atalian Special Forces."

# PART TWO
## THE CAPTURED PRINCESS

# CHAPTER 18

Not long-ago Isa was a retired soldier pleading to the King for her village and now she was the General of the Atalian Special Forces. Having the authority, Isa vowed to make changes, vowed to her people to protect them better. She bowed before Orion's father pledging her alliance to Atalia and to the royal family swearing to uphold the royal oath.

Orion beamed with pride standing next to his mother and father while Victoria, Laura, Benjamin, and the rest of the court as the King swore her in. Isa was ready to fully immerse herself into her new role.

She learned quickly how many meetings she was required to attend with the King and Orion. However, her new role made it hard for her to spend personal time with Orion.

Fall turned into winter as the preparations for the Ball

continued. The castle became decorated with winter celebrations. As Isa sat in her new office, she stopped what she was doing to turn around and watch the first snow flurries fall from her window behind her. Fully dressed in her new navy-blue military uniform, Isa was trying to finish her paperwork for the day.

Laura and Victoria surprised Isa and decorated her new office. Some of the winter decorations across the room look different in front of the stacks of paper and books organized across her desk. Placing her head in her hand, someone knocked on her door bringing her out of her focused trance.

"Come in," Isa said, signing one last paper before placing it on another stack.

"My General?" Orion smiled at Isa as he entered her office.

"My Prince." Isa grinned back at him as Orion closed the door behind him.

Isa stood in front of her desk leaning her body against it crossing her arms as Orion approached her. "I welcome your visits. Does your father need something from me?" Isa asked going to one of the bookshelves she had organized from her former commander. Archives and records adorned the shelves as Isa waited for Orion's answer.

"He requested everyone in the throne room for an advisory meeting, now," Orion said as Isa turned away from the bookcase nodding.

"Well, lead the way, my Prince," Isa teased Orion as he smiled back at her.

Arm in arm, they walked out of her office and into the castle hallway. In comfortable silence, they both walked through the castle before entering the stone throne room where everyone was waiting for them.

Isa found her assigned seat on the long table. The court and the other Generals, Lieutenants, and Captains took their appropriate seats as Isa waited for the King to address them.

"I have gathered you all here today to share some important news about our neighboring Kingdom, Zudora," the King said, leaning his hands against the table looking at everyone.

"A tough civil war has been going on for almost two decades now."

"What does this have to do with the Kingdom of

Atalia?" Lord Bryan asked from across Isa.

A chorus of nods and agreements filled the room as the King leaned back and started pacing explaining himself.

"More and more citizens are gathering on the streets rioting and demanding the release of the Zudoran heir to the throne. Queen Maziar captured and imprisoned Princess Safiya a month ago. The new Queen is blocking valuable trading routes between our kingdoms." Orion's father explained pointing to different parts of the map.

The King continued. "Ever since Queen Maziar took over the crown, she cut off all ties with Zudora's previous allies, including us. We've gained some intelligence from supporters and refugees that have crossed the border. If she finds out that we are sending our army over the border it could give her cause to attack us," the King explained as Isa nodded.

"I can plan a rescue mission, my King," Isa added.

"Good thinking. However, we need enough soldiers here to defend the castle in case of an attack," The King added.

"What happened to the rest of the royal family?" A captain asked from next to Isa.

"Well, the Von Brandt family were originally in power, but Maziar overthrew their King after his second marriage to Lady Helena Rochat. Queen Maziar has been growing her dark army ever since the King's first wife. All we know about the previous Queen was that she is that the last descendant of the Bertocchi family mysteriously disappeared."

Isa froze at the King's words and the mentioning of the last name of the royal family .

The King continued "It would be an act of war to move into and rescue the Princess in Zudora. My son, however, has renegotiated a new peace treaty with the Kingdom of Endrancia and we have more allies at our disposal."

Isa stared at the wooden table in front of her. *The King had said Bertocchi. The same last name General Adrastus had called her right before he died. He also called her Princess.*

"General, would you like to add a possible plan to avoid war?" the King asked.

Isa looked up in shock not listening to Orion or the King and seeing everyone watching her confused.

Isa coughed. "I need a moment, my King. Will you

excuse me for a second?"

Isa stood up bowing at the King and Orion. Watching her go, Orion followed behind her out of the throne room and into the hallway. Leaning against the wall, Isa placed a hand on her forehead feeling a headache coming on. Looking down, she held her other hand to her face seeing it shake.

Taking a deep breath, she turned towards Orion. *I need to tell him what the Adrastus told me during the battle. He needs to know.*

"What's wrong?" Orion asked seriously.

Isa sighed leaning her head against the wall.

"I should have told you this. Before General Adrastus was about to die, he confessed something really important to me, something I have not mentioned to anyone," Isa started pushing herself off the wall and walking towards Orion who opened his arms accepting her into his embrace.

"He called me Princess Isa Bertocchi. I have a surname. I have a family crest."

"Wait, that's the same name as the rightful royal family in-," Orion said, adding all the pieces together.

"Ms. Whittle never mentioned to me anything about my surname. She said I didn't have one. But how did *he* know?"

"The General said he knew me better than I know myself," Isa whispered, looking at him desperately for answers. Feeling his hands rubbing her arms, Isa still couldn't relax her heart drumming against her chest.

"He was trying to distract you and make you lose your focus." Orion reassured her.

"I don't know Orion; I think he was pretty serious."

Suddenly, Isa groaned in pain as she touched her head making Orion stop and panic.

The steady rhythm of the ache in her head made the world around her spin. Orion's face blurred in Isa's vision as the pain exploded making her hold her head in her hands trying to ease the agony.

"Isa, what is happening to you? Isa, can you hear me?" Orion asked not knowing what to do, but she didn't answer him again as the pain grew worse.

Feeling woozy, everything started to wobble. She would have fallen if Orion hadn't caught her. Panicking, Orion lifted her limp body into his arms and carried her away, running to the healing ward. It felt like an eternity as Isa hissed in pain wanting to curl her body to stop the throbbing in her head not knowing what was happening to her.

Orion placed her on a bed and the feeling of a cool ointment on her head helped the pain die down. Her eyesight was still blurry, her body relaxed as different voices rose around her. Sweat trickled down her face as she blinked trying to focus on the voices around her, but she couldn't.

Isa closed her eyes, sending her into darkness.

⚬

Her eyes fluttering open, Isa reached up and touched her forehead, the aching in her head had ceased. The ointment had worked wonders. Fully awake, Isa looked around and grinned seeing Orion on her right and Laura on her left.

"I'm glad you're awake," Orion chuckled as Laura nodded in agreement. Smiling weakly, Isa carefully sat up still feeling the effects of her episode. With Orion's help, she winced as she looked around.

Holding a cup of water to her, Laura gave her a sad grin as Isa accepted it. Nodding her head in thanks, Isa took a drink of the freshwater letting out a sigh before addressing them both.

"What happened to me?"

Rubbing her back, Orion spoke.

"You fell into my arms in pain. You kept holding your head, and I didn't know what to do so I brought you here," he said. "Tell me what's wrong."

Orion was too good at reading her and he knew something was up. Isa sighed knowing she had to tell.

"I've had some headaches lately since I defeated General Adrastus."

Orion raised his eyebrows at her.

"I didn't want to worry you or anyone," Isa whispered looking down at their interlocked hands. Orion squeezed them leaning forward, showing her that he was still there.

"We are all here for you. You have people that you can turn to for support. Victoria, Laura, or myself. Don't deal with this alone. You scared us," Orion pleaded as Isa nodded in understanding looking at him.

"Where is Victoria?" Isa asked as she turned to Laura

expecting her to have the answer.

"She's in the library finding more information for me." Laura said. Isa let out a chuckle raising an eyebrow jokingly. "While you were asleep, we noticed something strange appear on your arm."

Flipping through the book Laura had in her hand, she tried to find the right page.

"What? Is the dark magic spreading in me? The same one that killed Moore's husband?" She asked worriedly.

"Isa, you must have triggered some kind of reaction in your magical ability after you killed your former commander, which caused you to have these bad headaches. They were manifestations of your power. They were growing pains." Laura explained as Isa was silent, not knowing what to say next.

Isa panicked. *Did I lose my only magic? Would I still be able to talk to animals? My true magic?*

Hearing Orion move, Isa turned towards him watching as he reached up to her arm. Rolling up her sleeve, Orion stopped right above her elbow. Once Orion's hand moved out of the way, Isa finally looked down at her arm.

Very thin black markings wrapped around her forearm

down to her wrist like a black river. Curling in intricate and geometric designs, Isa thought the markings were very pretty, but she was confused about what they signified. There were circles or holes in the pattern that seemed like something would fit there.

"What are they?" Isa asked, mesmerized, tracing the lines with her fingers. Laura sighed, lifting and placing the big dusty book in Isa's lap as she pointed to the page that held a drawing of Isa's marking. Intrigued, she leaned in closer to the pages and touched the design symbol.

"Orion told us about your last name and he asked us to do some research. Your markings," Laura pointed to the design on the book, "are hereditary."

"The Bertocchi family is one of the oldest houses that dates back centuries," Orion added as Laura glanced at him.

"Isa, they were masters of dark magic," Laura added. "Because of this, they were persccuted and hunted so they knew that the only way to survive was to weave themselves into society, rebranding themselves. However, the one power they couldn't weed out of their ancestry was blood magic." Laura concluded looking down at Isa.

"Some records showed that the Bertocchi family married into the house of Von Brandt, the family that ruled Zudora. The last descendant disappeared twenty-one years ago," Orion added slowly as Isa swallowed before glancing at both confused finally starting to understand.

"Your mother was the last of the Bertocchi family and was the Queen of Zudora, making you the first born and rightful true heir to the Zudoran throne."

# CHAPTER 19

"You would have to claim the throne at some point," Orion said sitting on top of her bed while Isa paced in front of him. Orion was worried about her claim to the Zudoran throne because Isa would leave Deval and he would lose her.

"But I don't want to claim the throne! I want to stay here in Atalia. What about Princess Safiya?" Isa said as she moved to rub her eyes.

"What we know is that she's been captured by Queen Maziar. We think that the only reason the Queen Maziar has kept the Princess alive is to gain the support from the local villagers. Despite the riots, she managed to stay in power. Isa, as you know, we cannot interfere otherwise we would start a war. My kingdom wants peace and now that Endrancia and us are allies, we can't risk breaking this new peace treaty," Orion added.

Sighing, Isa nodded rubbing her forehead knowing that he was right. "Does this make Princess Safiya my sister?" Isa whispered, grinning. "I have a family; I have a blood sister?"

He took a deep breath pausing for a second before answering. He really wanted to be the voice of reason. Isa had the claim to the Zudora throne, but if she made a public statement, it would only be a matter of time before Isa became a target.

"Look Isa, the Ball is next week, you just pledged your alliance as the General to Atalia. Let's plan our next move after the Ball is finished and after my coronation. I will support your decision and if you decide to claim your throne, we can invade Zudora and fight the Queen," Orion spoke softly, trying to compromise.

Turning over her shoulder to look at him, Isa blinked, nodding slowly in agreement as she sighed knowing that he was right. Laying her head on Orion's stomach, Isa looked up at the stone ceilings. Feeling Orion stroke her hair gently, she sighed in comfort as she relaxed.

"I can't believe it. I went from being an orphan who knew nothing about their parents to knowing who my parents were and having a younger sister!" Isa scuffed, throwing her hands in the air.

Orion smiled gently and kissed her forehead before moving to her lips while placing his hand behind her head. Deepening the kiss, Isa smiled into it as she took a breath. Looking at Orion's vibrant blue eyes, she knew one thing for certain: she was happy to have Orion by her side.

The next day, Isa could not stop thinking about her family and her sister. She was obsessed about finding more about her blood magic. She did find that blood magic was an old but deadly magic. It seemed this knowledge was a well kept secret of the Bertocchi family. She also found more interesting information about the marriage records which proved that her family had married into the Von Brandt Royal bloodline.

Isa never would have thought that she would gain more magical abilities passed down from her bloodline. Magic was inheritable, but some was taught. Truth magic, for example, Isa learned it during her time as a soldier in the special forces.

However, she was born with the ability to talk to certain

animals which she deduced was inherited. Her mother must have had the blood magic while her father had the ability to talk to animals. Her father must have known about her mother's blood magic otherwise, Isa could have died as an infant. The amount of magical bloodline passed down to some offspring was too much for them. Many children died at birth because of the power given by both families.

*How did I manage to overcome and not die? How did my sister manage to survive? Does she know I even exist?*

A knock on her office door distracted Isa from her thoughts as Isa cleared her throat.

"Come in," Isa stated.

"Hi Victoria," Isa said as Victoria closed the door behind her coming up to Isa's desk.

"Isa, I'm glad you're feeling better," Victoria commented. Isa nodded weakly, sighing.

"I'm sure it must have been a shock for you to find out about your family last name," Victoria continued. " If I would have known about your surname and family, I would have told you."

Victoria was one of the first girls at Ms. Whittle's Orphanage. She probably would have known about it and would have told her. Isa trusted her.

"I know, you would," Isa smiled weakly. Victoria nodded happily with her answer before leaning back onto her desk again.

"I came to tell you that the Ball is in a week. Have you picked out a gown yet?"

"No, I haven't."

"You'll need to wear something perfect. Something befitting of royalty, if you know what I mean," Victoria whispered winking at Isa. "I want Orion to look at you and be so amazed that he will literally faint at the sight of you!"

Isa let out a hearty chuckle.

"You are coming with me, now."

Before Isa could ask, Victoria grabbed Isa's hand and dragged her out of her office.

"Victoria, where are you taking me?" Isa asked, smiling as Victoria led her through the castle.

Passing the training grounds and through the red clad carpeted hallways, Isa laughed as they passed Orion on the way who looked at them confused. Isa shrugged her shoulders as they ran past him. Victoria didn't answer Isa's question until they arrived at a new door.

"We found the royal tailor for you!" Victoria said as she pushed Isa into the room.

<hr>

After finishing her morning with the royal tailor, Isa decided it was a good idea to explore Deval with Victoria and Laura.

Weaving through the crowd of people, the girls could not stop talking about who was taking them to the Ball. They were laughing with each other as they roamed around the market. Picking up some fresh pastries from the bakers they ate as they started heading back to the castle.

Isa needed this time. She needed to get out of the castle for a couple of hours to calm her mind about everything and get some fresh air. Isa relished how calm it was to stroll through the town like this with her friends.

She did not want to think about the impending fate of Zudora and her own destiny. *I don't want the crown of Zudora. It belongs to my sister Safiya. I was born and raised here in Atalia. This is my home. I will defend and fight for the Kingdom of Atalia and for my people.*

⊰◦⊱

After having another fun day exploring Deval with Laura and Victoria, Isa made her way to her bedroom despite having spent more time in Orion's than her own. Slowly peeling off her uniform and placing her weapons on her desk with a clang, Isa glanced at the glass window in her room. Stepping towards it, the start of the sunset cast the white snowy hills of Atalia a soft orange and pink.

Jumping towards her door, she immediately went towards Orion's door quickly pushing it open making him sit up in bed with surprise and shock. His curtains were drawn as Orion looked at her sleepily.

"Isa?" He groggily rubbed his eyes looking at her.

"Orion, get up!"

Wanting to have some fun, Isa stepped to the side of Orion's bed as she started patting his leg above the covers trying to make him more awake.

"Come on I want to take you somewhere please," Isa pleaded as she kept patting his leg. Letting out a breath,

Orion laid back down on his bed with a huff looking up at her.

"Now?" He asked placing his arm over his eyes. Isa nodded humming tugging at his hand as Orion slowly sat up again with a groan.

"And here I was thinking I would be able take a quick nap before dinner," he chuckled smiling at Isa as she shook her head grasping his hand.

"Come on!"

"Alight alright, give me a second," Orion laughed as Isa released him letting Orion get out of bed.

Once he had put his boots on and a thicker coat like her, Isa grabbed his hand again and rushed him out of his room. With haste, she led Orion though the hallways of the castle and to the back part of the castle away from the main areas. Going up a random hidden spiral staircase, Orion didn't know where he was going for once. He had never come to this part of the castle before, but he couldn't help but notice the garrison barracks across the stone wall. Ignoring it as Isa led him up the staircase, they got to the top of the tower.

Isa released his hand and stood in front of a small wooden door. Looking back at him, Isa smiled before pushing open the door to the roof of the castle. Thankfully, the sun had melted the snow on the roof, but the moss covered the tiles. As Isa climbed up and started walking, Orion crawled through the door.

"Where are we?" He asked wiping his sleeves as Isa sat down with view of the setting sun over the city of Deval. Hearing her silence, Orion walked up to her and sat down next to her following her line of sight.

Seeing the white smooth pristine rolling hills of Atalia and the frozen lake, the sun kept the landscape lit for a little bit longer. The sky was a beautiful mixture of purples and oranges that reflected in the ice covered water of the lake.

"What is this?" Orion whispered looking at Isa beside him.

As the soft breeze whisked strands of rich dark brown hair from her face, Isa took a deep relaxing before she answered.

"When I was in the forces, this was the only place I was able to come to when I was in the barracks. I used to sneak into the castle and come here when I wanted to be alone after drills or just get away from people in general. I used to love coming here on clear summer evenings. I know it's a bit chilly today but it's a clear sky and the stars are magnificent. No one knows about this place except for me," Isa said glancing at Orion who grinned at her softly.

"Two people."

"Hm?"

"I already knew about this place," Orion chuckled as Isa gasped dramatically.

"You knew? Why didn't you say anything?"

Grinning, Orion answered.

"Well you were excited to show me but now it's even more special because you're here with me."

With that, Isa smiled nudging him.

Turning back towards the landscape, they both watched the sun set behind the hills and the lights of the city start to appear enjoying each other's company. Even with the sun behind the hills, there was still a bit of light left to see as the street lights sprinkled across the city.

Hoping Orion wasn't bored, Isa turned her head towards him getting a good glance at him. The breeze rustled his wheat colored curls and he just looked so at peace watching the scene before him.

Then Isa noticed something.

Smiling, she reached a hand out to his face as he turned towards her with a questioning glance towards her hand.

"You shaved?" Isa said bringing her hand back down having noticed the little scabs around his jaw. Smiling, Orion lifted his own hand to touch the smoothness of his jaw.

"Mhm," he nodded as Isa smiled at him. Moving his eyes to the side before meeting her again, Orion lifted his eyebrows.

"What?"

"Nothing," Isa grinned. Orion shook his head chuckling to himself.

"I know I know; I look like I'm eighteen again. Benjamin keeps telling me I have a baby face," Orion chuckled gesturing towards his cheeks.

"I can see that," Isa replied as she laughed along. Putting his weight on his hands behind him, Orion leaned towards Isa.

"Funny enough it was on my mother's request for the ball tomorrow."

A sharp pang rang through Isa's chest. The ball. It was coming up so soon. Swallowing, she grinned.

"Well I think you still look very handsome." Isa added looking down and playing with the moss that covered the roof tiles.

"Yeah?" Orion smiled looking at Isa as she nodded.

After picking at the moss for a bit, she slowly lowered herself to lay down on the tiles to look up at the stars in the darkening sky. Thankfully, her navy blue general uniform coat kept her warm as she looked up at the twinkling stars appearing in the sky. Seeing this, Orion then joined her as they laid side by side looking up at the glittering night. It reminded the both of them about their journeys camping out in the woods underneath the same sky.

Orion shivered a bit before speaking.

"In all fairness, I think you are going to look amazing tomorrow," he said turning his head to look at Isa as he grasped her hand interlocking their fingers at their side.

"Oh hush your flattery Orion. I've never been to a ball before," Isa smiled giving his hand a slight squeeze.

"Well I still think you'd look absolutely beautiful even if you went in your army uniform," Orion whispered watching her. At his comment, Isa turned her head to look at him to see him softly grinning back at her.

"Thanks, ever the charmer."

"Damn right."

Isa and Orion laughed as they watched each other relaxing underneath the blackening sky.

"Do I look older with stubble though?" Orion said stroking his jaw with a smile as Isa slapped his shoulder in playfulness.

"Hmm let me think."

Orion kept smoothing his hand over his jaw dramatically at her making her laugh.

"Stop! Let your general make her decision," Isa chuckled as she stuck her tongue out between her teeth giggling.

"I'm older then you and I technically outrank you," Orion played along.

"Respectfully shut up your highness."

Calming themselves down from their laughter, they both looked back up at the stars again. Feeling his thumb stroking her knuckles, Isa closed her eyes smelling the fresh air and the slight chill in the air. It felt nice for her to show Orion this spot, now she didn't have to be alone whenever she wanted to come here. Plus it was nice to have Orion all to herself.

Hearing rustling, Isa opened her eyes turning towards him as Orion opened his mouth to speak.

"But seriously, thank you for showing me this," he said.

Smiling softly, she went back to gazing up at the sky.

"I haven't had the chance to come back here again and I guess my suitor deserves to know about this place," Isa smirked.

Orion turned to his side propping himself up on his elbow looking at her. Reaching a hand to move some stray hairs away from Isa's face, Orion gently smiled down at her.

"I really can't wait to see you tomorrow night," he whispered leaning in closer to her face.

"Yeah?" Isa breathed as her heart rate spiked.

"Mhm," he nodded leaning in closer.

Isa, impatient, grabbed the back of his head to push his lips into hers. Smiling into the kiss, Orion leaned back ever so slightly, but Isa wanted to keep going and pouted when he pulled back.

"Desperate are we?" Orion smirked tracing a finger

across her jaw. Feeling her cheeks burn up, she shook her head.

"Oh shut up," she smirked slapping his chest releasing his hair.

"Your family is probably expecting us soon anyway," Isa said sitting up and wiping her clothes off.

"One more though."

"Huh-," Isa began as she turned her head towards Orion before he grabbed both of her cheeks pressing another kiss to her lips. Titling her head to deepen it, she could hear the start of a moan from Orion's mouth. Slowly coming out of it, he opened his eyes stroking her cheekbones with his thumbs. Examining Isa's face, he leaned her head down to press a kiss to her forehead.

Isa smiled warmly watching him.

"Ok now we can go," Orion nodded releasing Isa's face and standing up holding out a hand for her.

Grinning, Isa grasped it as he helped her stand up. As they left the roof, Isa felt the start of butterflies in her stomach in anticipation of the ball tomorrow. Taking a deep breath, she looked down at their interlocked hands and smiled at Orion's back.

With him by her side, she knew everything would be alright.

# CHAPTER 20

The day of the Ball arrived and the castle was in an organized chaos. Servants were rushing around the place making sure the preparations were in order as they finished placing the final decoration in the throne room for the big celebration. Guests had filled up all of the rooms Isa noticed as more and more guests started arriving.

Thankfully, her office was on the other side of the castle near the barracks. Isa had stayed in her office ignoring the footsteps rumbling through the hallways. As it was a day of festivities, Isa gave some officers a day off but kept most of the guards.

Looking down at her desk, Isa started reading the letter she received from Ms. Whittle asking her how she was doing at the castle. Ms. Whittle told Isa how the children were doing at the Orphanage and that everyone was safe.

There were no more deaths reported. Isa knew that Ayden would have flown to her if he noticed anything unusual.

*There would be a lot of important people at the Ball tonight. I need to make a good impression. I am the General of the Atalian Special Forces. I would need to talk to the leaders of the other kingdoms and find out more what is happening with the civil unrest in Zudora.*

A knock on her office door made Isa jump and look up to see Victoria with Laura closely behind her. Shocked, Isa watched them stride to her desk both in robes with their hair in towels in the middle of getting ready for the Ball.

"Isa, what are you still doing here!" Victoria squealed grabbing Isa's arms lifting her up from her chair. "It's time to get ready for the Ball! It's in two hours!" Victoria dragged Isa out of the office and into the hallway where they dodged people with Laura behind them.

Meanwhile Orion was pacing around his room rubbing his hands together as Benjamin, with his unruly black hair combed back, sat in one of the chairs in the corner watching his cousin. Benjamin had a slight smirk on his face seeing Orion this nervous. The tailor was trying to put some last-minute touches on his coat but kept failing as Orion walked away. Seeing his cousin and friend so tense, Benjamin spoke.

"Orion?" Benjamin said his green eyes moving back and forth at Orion's pacing figure. He finally turned and stopped right in front of Benjamin.

"I can't Ben." Orion rubbed his eyes in worry going back to pacing. Benjamin sighed and then chuckled at his friend's red face.

"What's the worst that could happen? You could panic and not be able to get the words out." Benjamin asked.

Immediately, Orion turned to his friend frowning as Benjamin cackled. The Prince was silent interlocking his hands thinking.

"Maybe I should talk to her first before-," Orion stated starting to walk to the door but Benjamin jumped up in panic and blocked him.

"No, wait till the Ball. Everything will work out fine."

"I supposed you are right," Orion smiled imagining.

<hr>

"Come on, the Ball is starting soon," Isa smiled at her friends.

Laura had her naturally straight red long hair down and was wearing a flowy dark purple dress while Victoria had her blonde curls in an updo and was wearing a body contouring pastel pink dress. They both looked beautiful.

Victoria went to a long white box that was on Isa's bed. She hummed and nodded pulling the ribbon open before opening the box. Reaching into it, Victoria gently held up the most magnificent dress Isa had ever seen. She was speechless.

Isa' dress sparkled like the stars shimmering on a vibrant dark blue. *The colors of the flag of Atalia.* There are black designs embroidered all over the blue laced right sleeve.

The dress flowed freely across Victoria arms like silk as she rested it in her hands walking to Isa's side as Isa examined the dress in detail.

"Do you like it?" Victoria smiled seeing Isa's wide eyes and open mouth.

"I love it!" Isa clapped in happiness as she stood up excited and ready to put it on.

Isa noticed that only her right arm was covered with the blue lace. Her markings were visible on her left forearm. Giving her friends a twirl, the dress seemed to lift up and sparkle like stars.

Smoothing down the dress, Isa walked to look at herself in the mirror. The three girls looked like nobility.

Laura, Victoria, and Isa all walked through the hallways towards the throne room. It was agony for Isa as they strolled through the maze of the castle in silence. Isa, in the middle, had her arms wrapped around her friends Laura and Victoria.

Taking a deep breath, Isa stepped forward as the footmen leaned to open the doors. The music and bright colors burst into Isa's vision as the doors fully opened. People were all dancing together in circles around the throne room. Isa tightened her hold on her friends' arms. As they walked into the room, the crowd parted for them. The dancers stopped to stare at the girls. Scanning the many faces around them, Isa tightened her grip.

It seemed that all eyes were on the three of them.

The King and Queen were standing gracefully on the throne platform and welcoming the guests with Orion at their side. Orion could not stop staring at Isa when she walked in the room. Feeling his gaze, she grinned at him happy to see him.

Orion's blonde hair was combed back. Isa couldn't help but feel warmth spread to her cheeks before noticing that he too was wearing a navy-blue ceremonial uniform. Orion started walking towards Isa, Laura and Victoria. Seeing him approaching, they released Isa and pushed her forward.

"May I have this dance, Isa?" Orion said smiling and bowing down holding out a hand for her to take.

Isa smiled and accepted putting her hand into his. Orion grasped her hand gently and smiled guiding her to the middle of the dance floor. The music started playing once again as Isa stepped into a circle with Orion. As they danced, Isa managed to catch glimpses from the corner of her eye at Victoria and Laura dancing with their own partners. That made Isa smile.

"Where did you learn our Atalian dance?" Orion asked twirling Isa around him. Letting go of his hands, she answered smirking.

"All those long hour lessons I had with your mother. She taught me how to dance," she said as they continued dancing around each other.

All too quickly, the music ended. Taking her hand,

Orion pulled Isa away leading her through the crowd.

"Come with me. I have something to show you," he said leading Isa out of the room.

<hr>

Orion gently led her into a secret passageway through the back of the castle before he stopped at an old wooden door. It looked older than most of the modern doors in the castle. Looking at her, Orion grinned before slowly pushing the door open for her.

The room was filled with bright pink flowers and all sorts of green plants growing along the lattices surrounding the edge of the room. They hung across the ceiling making the room fill with petals. Ivy hung down to the floor as glass mirrors peaked through them. Isa glanced at her reflection before speaking.

"This secret room has been in our castle for centuries and was only used by the royals. I don't know how the magic works but the room becomes whatever you need it to be. You showed me your favorite place, it's time to show you mine," Orion said stepping closer to Isa, his focus completely on her.

"My mother brought me here when I was a young boy and I wanted to bring you here too," he added inching closer.

"Isa-," Orion started but took a deep breath as she looked up at him waiting for him to continue.

"I never thought I would find someone in this lifetime, but here you are, in my world," Orion said placing a stray hair behind Isa's ear.

"Orion, please. I can't-," Isa started looking down shaking her head trying to step back but then she felt Orion's finger on her chin, lifting it gently.

"I thought I would never be a good future King like my father is. Because you made me realize that Atalia is only as great as their leaders. I can't rule without you by my side, Isa. The finest leader I have ever known." Orion swallowed, thinking about his next words.

"Orion, I believe in you and I am honored to serve Atalia." Isa took in a deep breath as she tried to continue but she stopped when she saw Orion kneel in front of her.

"Will you marry me, Isa Bertocchi? My future Queen." Orion whispered stroking Isa's chin with his hand.

Isa remained silent while tears were appearing in her

eyes.

With Isa's hesitation, Orion did not know how to react. He continued "If this is not what you want, then tell me-."

Isa stopped him with a finger on his mouth. His eyes widened watching her carefully.

"I accept."

Orion was speechless.

Before he could open his mouth to respond to Isa, a rumble noise started shaking them. At the same time a chill run through Isa's body. A strange energy rippled through her body. A dark feeling that was crawling and spreading inside her. Isa gripped to Orion as quickly as she could.

Grabbing Isa's hand, Orion ran out of the room and back to the main area of the castle. As they stepped into the main hallway, guards ran past them as Orion watched them in astonishment not knowing what was happening.

Orion pulled one of the guards towards him.

"What is happening?" He commanded at the posted guard.

"Your Royal Highness, I am so sorry. The King has been

injured. My Prince and my General, glad to see that you are both safe," he said.

Orion's eyes widened like he had been punched.

Isa and Orion burst through the throne room doors. Isa immediately covered her mouth in shock. They were immediately bombarded with the image of Orion's father dead body on the floor in a pool of blood and Orion's mother weeping and crying.

Near the King's body and where the Queen was, there was another woman standing near them. Her hair was as black as a moonless night and she wore a dark purple dress that seemed to be floating in an empty abyss around her. Isa could feel the waves of magic coming off her.

"Father!" Orion cried out. Isa stopped him with her arm watching this new person carefully.

"Just the person I was looking for. William's heir," she said sarcastically walking around in a circle.

"Who are you and what are you doing here?" Orion commanded Isa was standing next to him making sure he was protected.

"I'm Queen Maziar, your Highness."

Isa's eyes widened. She was the Queen that had taken

over Zudora and was holding Princess Safiya hostage.

Through the corner of his eyes, Orion saw that one of the guards was waving and holding his bow. He ran as fast as he could to grab it. However, once it was in his hands, he failed to produce the light arrows. Queen Maziar saw Orion's futile attempt and she sent a pillar of shadows towards Orion making him fly to the side of the room.

Isa frowned at the Queen and then looked back to make sure Orion was safe. Her priority was to protect the Prince.

"A light sorcerer that can't produce his arrows yet. So sad."

*This is the same magic I saw during my combat with General Adrastus.*

"You, where can I find General Adrastus?" Maziar asked pointing her boney finger at Isa who watched her sternly.

"He's dead," Isa stated. Queen Maziar titled her head at her answer scoffing.

"He isn't dead. My personal scout can do better than that." Maziar laughed.

Isa's hands tingled and shook in anticipation. She ready

to fight.

"You're not afraid of me?" Maziar asked. "Who are you?"

Knowing that everyone in the ballroom was listening closely to what she has to say, Isa cleared her throat and spoke.

"I am Isa, General of the Special Forces. I am the one who killed General Adrastus taking his place as commander," Isa said clenching her fists taking a step closer to the Queen Maziar.

"I don't believe you. Wait," Maziar burst out laughing. "You're serious. Hold on. The General mentioned your name. Isa. Isa. Hm. I thought he killed you already and yet here you are in the flesh and blood."

When she said the word blood, Isa's hands shook even more and her marking making her wince. Isa tried to surpass the urge to use her new magic. Queen Maziar glanced down at Isa's arm before Isa could hide it behind her back.

"Let me see what you have behind you." Maziar started walking towards Isa. She glanced down at Isa's hidden arm looking back up at her.

"You have the Power of the Erythro.  There was only one royal that could wield blood magic before you-. It cannot be." Maziar furrowed her eyebrows.

"What's your name?"

"My name is Isa Bertocchi."

Maziar reeled back in shock finally piercing together the puzzle as she pointed an accusatory finger at Isa.

"Bertocchi. Your mother took everything from me. She stole my crown!" Maziar slammed her fist down and stomped her foot as an angry child having a tantrum. Then shadows started bursting from her body. When she finally stopped and calmed herself down, she continued.

"King Daniel chose Miss Rosa Bertocchi as his Queen. He was supposed to marry me! Me! I put in the hard work, I put in the time, and what do I get? NOTHING! And then he married again, and who does he choose? Not me! He told me 'Maziar, you aren't right for the kingdom' It was all your mother's fault I didn't become queen in the first place! I'm glad I killed him!" She screamed at Isa.

*She is very dangerous. She has a temper. She is wielding more power than General Adrastus did. I won't be intimi-*

*dated by her power. I need to protect Orion and his mother.*

"Now, now this is too good to pass. I can end the Dawn Monarchy right now but I won't today. " Maziar's mood shifted back to normal.

"I won't harm anybody else unless if I don't get what I want. Here is the deal, I want the true heir to the Zudoran throne or I can kill Prince Orion-," Queen Maziar said tapping a finger on her pronounced sickly pale chin.

Isa stepped forward and shouted. "I'm the one you want. As you said, I am the heir of Zudora." Isa started gesturing towards herself.

"No, Isa you can't!" Orion said before some guards stopped him.

"On one condition, you have to promise to leave Atalia immediately and take your army of skeletons if I come with you?" Isa added. Maziar kept on thinking as she hummed.

Isa turned to look at him from over her shoulder. Orion tried to get out of the guards' grasp as she looked at him sadly.

"Alright." Queen Maziar said.

"NO!" Orion screamed and finally managed to get out

of the arms of the guards. He jumped forward and ran straight to get his bow again that laid on the ground.

"Orion don't!" Isa pleaded with him. She didn't want him to be killed. She knew he couldn't produce the light arrows.

Orion knelt down and grabbed the bow lifting it towards Maziar who scoffed at him. He tried again by pulling back his bow and this time a white light energy arrow started forming against the bowstring. Isa's eyes widened.

Once it was fully constructed, his fingers released and the arrow pierced through the air screeching towards Maziar with great speed and accuracy. She saw it coming and managed to stop the arrow with her shadow magic.

Isa's sacrifice was the catalyst Orion needed to trigger his power. He finally understood his father's words.

"You missed. Keep practicing, just keep practicing, young Prince." Maziar cackled.

⚔

Guards bowed as Orion walked through the throne room doors. Stopping in front of him, Benjamin looked up at his cousin. Noticing Orion's red and wet eyes, he grabbed his shoulders.

"Orion, what happened?" Benjamin asked in shock.

"My father is dead and Isa is gone. She took her." Orion voiced cracked barely breathing trying to contain himself.

"Who?"

"Queen Maziar took Isa. She sacrificed herself for us all, to save my Kingdom."

Benjamin went to kneel down but before he could do that Orion stopped him wrapping his arms around Benjamin's desperately.

'Long live the King' echoed from within throne room.

# CHAPTER 21

Maziar had ignored Isa most of the journey to Zudora. Not before she managed to dehumanize Isa as much as she could. Tearing her dress, cutting her hair, dragging her along in chains behind her carriage. Isa stayed strong and didn't complain.

Once they reached the capital, Isa noticed the faces of the people of Zudora. They looked miserable and angry as they parted to let Maziar's carriage in shaking their heads at sight of Isa. Isa could see their pitiful glances hearing their hushed whispers as she drudged through the mud. Wooden and stone buildings surrounded the main castle as ashy ruins were sprinkled throughout the capital.

Suddenly, the carriage came to a rolling stop. It gave Isa an opportunity to rest her legs as they were tingling in exhaustion. Wiggling her toes, she tried to get some warmth back to them. They had stopped right in front of the dark and looming castle. She noticed the lifeless structure before them, the skeleton of a once prosperous kingdom.

A good crowd of people had gathered in front of the carriage. They were intrigued at the new person in chains. Stepping onto the wet gravel, Maziar walked around and unhooked Isa's chain and yanked her forward like an animal to show to the crowd.

"People of Fyre, look upon this girl for she is the last of the Bertocchi family and the true heir of Zudora." Maziar was clearly enjoying seeing Isa's chained up in front of her.

"We want the Princess. Release Princess Safiya!" A man yelled and the people around him agreed shouting in unison 'Princess Safiya'.

As people started getting close to the carriage with their fists raised, Maziar gritted her teeth at them before shooting a hand out, palm facing the ground. Shadowy skeleton warriors burst from the ground and started corralling the people making them go silent in fear.

*Was Queen Maziar a necromancer?*

"Your precious Princess is safe and sound inside the

castle," she spat.

As the broken wooden doors of the dark icy castle opened, a skeleton guard came up running and immediately bowed to Maziar.

"Take her away." Maziar said throwing the chains to him.

"Right away, my Queen," he said in a gravelly voice tugging at the chain for Isa to follow him.

The skeleton guard led her through the halls of the castle where her mother used to live. Seeing the lifeless empty hallways of what used to be a great castle, flags burned and pillars crumbling, Isa realized that Maziar lived alone. Only the army of skeletons and the shadows obeyed her. Isa thought the dark Queen had killed everyone else in power that had supported the Von Brandts.

The skeleton guard was taking her to the dungeons.

What surprised Isa the most was the of noise and commotion she caused when they walked passed the big wooden door to the prison. Rows upon rows of cages were lined with griffins, unicorns and other magical creatures. The voices of all these creatures seemed to scream inside her head all at once but Isa kept going looking straight ahead.

Passing the cages, Isa wondered. Why did Queen Maziar have for all of these creatures in cages? What is she planning to do with them? *Some of these creatures are from the wastelands.*

Suddenly the clanging noises stopped as the creatures watched her. Their heads followed Isa as the guard took her to one of the cave prisons caves. He opened the metal door. Once she stepped inside, the guard locked the jail door, her metal chains around her wrists vanished into thin air.

The cave was dark with only the light coming from the jail doors.

As memories of the time she spent in prison came flushing to her mind, Isa's heartbeat suddenly intensified. Slumping against the rock wall, she curled herself into her body hyperventilating. Looking up as she panted, her vision blurred. Najia's voice came into her head. Isa went into deep silence and meditation.

*What can I see?*
*Rock. Bars. Darkness. Hippogriff. Dust.*
*Her breathing slowed down.*

*What can I hear?*

*The voices of the creatures locked up in the cages. Her heartbeat. Water droplets. Clanging of the metal cages.*

*What can I feel?*

*My fingers and toes are cold. The dryness of the rock wall pressing against my skin. My hair is drying up.*

Taking a deep breath, Isa looked around her. Lifting herself from the rock wall, she stretched her arms and her legs before a voice interrupted her silence.

*"Friend or foe? Who are you?"*

Isa heard this voice in her head. When she turned around, Isa saw a young dragon curled into one of the corners looking at her with big bright green eyes.

Dragons were a rarity. Isa had never seen one before. This dragon couldn't have been much taller than Isa's waist, their white scales barely illuminating in the dim light. Carefully, lowering herself onto the rock floor, she sat down crisscrossed in front of the young dragon who looked at her curiously.

"I am a friend. My name is Isa," she said waiting for the dragon to approach her. Slowly, he stepped towards her.

*"You can understand me?"*

Isa hummed and nodded.

As the dragon stepped towards the light, Isa could distinguish it was a young male dragon because of the little bumps of horns on his head. He was a rare almost extinct Atalian dragon breed called a *Lightfrill.* These dragons needed full sunlight to grow into their adult heights. They were the ones that developed light sorcery and used the sun to harness their power. They lived in the Western regions of Atalia near the Endrancia border, by the deserts.

"Yes, I can," Isa said.

*"That's great! My name is Myran! My new friend, so happy!"* He started doing circles around her happily.

"Are you Isa? The General of the Special Forces of Atalia?"

Standing up with Myran beside her, Isa tried to find where the voice was coming from. It was too dark in the cave. A flame appeared near a hole between the jail next to her.

Seeing the flame, Isa rushed to the hole seeing the small spark of light coming from the hand of a human. The fire glowed their faces as Isa immediately noticed the fire emblem on their neck. A slight orange and yellow flame had conjured in her hand. She had fire magic.

"Who you are?" Isa asked politely. The girl looked at Isa through the hole in the rock with her blue eyes and freckles across her face.

"I am Safiya," she smiled sadly.

"Princess Safiya? You're my sister," Isa stated in surprise.

"What do you mean I am your... sister?" Safiya asked confused.

"I'm Isa Bertocchi and the last of the Bertocchi Family. You and I are sisters. I am so happy to meet you. You need to tell me everything about my father and what you remember from those days."

"You are my father's first child?"

"Yes I am."

Safiya gave Isa a small smile.

"He died honorably trying to protect the capital from that witch. He loved your mother, but after the siege he married my mother. I was born a year later. He would tell me stories about the Bertocchi family and what they did for the continent."

Isa grinned.

"I heard what you did in Atalia," she said holding the flame steady in her hand.

"Who told you?"

"The guards, sometimes if you listen closely, they speak to each other. Most of them are under Maziar's control and know what is happening around her," Safiya answered.

*"Tell me, tell me. What did you do?"* Myran asked curiously as Isa turned to answer him, knowing that Safiya couldn't understand him.

"To answer your question Myran, I came here with Maziar to protect the lives of Prince Orion and his mother."

"And you scarified yourself for Atalia to save them." Safiya clarified as if it was common knowledge. Isa furrowed her eyebrows at her words.

"How do you know?"

"Word traveled quickly around here."

Looking around her jail, Isa noticed the double layers of iron bars that the other caves didn't have.

"Tell me, Safiya. Why does your cave have double layered iron?" Isa asked her.

"I melted the iron the first time when I was trying to escape. Then Maziar threatened to kill my people and the children of my kingdom. I stopped trying to escape and she just put in an extra layer."

"I am curious do you know what it is that Maziar planning with all of these creatures I saw in the cages near our cells?"

"Maziar runs a dark underground fighting ring where she sells creatures to anyone willing to pay a higher price for them. Maziar needed more money because taxing people can go so far. It's horrible and brutal, I know."

*"I don't want to fight."* Myran shivered from next to Isa. Isa turned to him.

"You're still young. You're a Lightfrill, Maziar doesn't want to hurt you because you are a rare dragon." Isa smiled at him trying to comfort him.

"Does Maziar make you fight?" Isa asked Safiya as she shook her head.

"No, because she knows I'll burn everything down." Safiya chuckled pausing. "But she takes me along to keep an eye on me ."

*Would Maziar have me fight?*

Orion was hunched over a table in the throne room. A map showed the positions of their troops all over Atalia and near the border of Zudora. Gripping the wood with his hands, he frowned looking up at Lieutenant Carya who was acting in Isa's place. Orion hadn't slept trying to find ways to rescue Isa from Zudora. But it was proving to be more difficult than he thought.

Orion was thrust into becoming King. He refused to continue with the coronation ceremony until Isa was back with him. He was helping his mother deal with his father's death and burial. Victoria and Laura were helping as much as they could.

"Your highness, General Bertocchi will find a way to escape," Lieutenant Carya said trying to reason with Orion.

Orion sighed knowing he was right. Thomas Carya knew Isa while she was in the forces and trusted her with his life. Thomas was the only one still left in the forces that remembered the mission in Endrancia.

"I don't want her to think that I'm not doing everything I can to bring her back," Orion said looking up at the acting General. Orion felt he could explode at any time.

"Your highness, with all due respect, if we try to rescue her, we will start a war with Zudora and face Maziar's wrath. Once you step over the border, it will be an act of invasion and you will be captured by her army of skeletons. Atalia cannot risk losing you. We've already lost your father; we can't lose you too," Lieutenant Carya finished swallowing watching the young king.

"Orion, we all saw how powerful Queen Maziar is. " He tried to reason with Orion, who slammed a hand on the table.

Orion took a deep breath as Lieutenant Carya gave the young King a look.

"What do you propose we do?"

"Send reinforcements to the villages close to Zudoran border. When General Bertocchi escapes, we will be waiting ready to help her once she crosses the border over into Atalia," he concluded.

"Very well. I give my permission, Lieutenant. Do it," Orion said waving him off. Lieutenant Carya bowed down and left the young King by himself.

Orion grasped the table trying to hold back the tears that were threatening to spill at any moment. He didn't want to leave Isa with Maziar. He knew making decision as the King would be hard, he knew he had duties and responsibilities for his people and kingdom.

His legs shook beneath him as Orion used the table to slowly lower himself to the ground placing his head in his hands. His heart drummed through his ears. He tried to compose himself and stop his breath from quickening. Running a hand through his hair, Orion looked around the empty throne room rubbing his eyes.

*The wait is killing me. Waiting for anything. Waiting for a messenger to come bursting through the doors with news that Isa had escaped.*

A faint tap on one of the stained-glass windows made Orion look up. Confused, he tilted his head up. He heard the flapping of wings and he noticed it was Ayden behind the glass. Eyes wide, Orion stepped around the table and rushed towards the window and pushed it to open.

"Ayden?" Orion asked as the falcon flew in.

Not understanding the falcon, Orion stretched out an arm for the bird to perch on. Once Ayden landed on his arms and settled, Orion looked at the falcon desperately.

"You probably heard what happened," Orion sighed sadly. "I don't know what to do, Ayden."

He hung his head low before Ayden kacked at him again. The falcon lifted his wings using his beak to point.

"Genius, Ayden! You can send a message to Isa? You know where she is," Orion exclaimed getting excited as the falcon nodded again. Moving Ayden to his shoulder, Orion ran out of the throne room and into the hallway determined. He ran past everyone. Even Benjamin and Laura looked at him confused, shrugging at each other as he dodged passed them. Bursting into his father's study, Orion wrote out a message on a loose piece of parchment.

Orion signed it and rolled it up so that Ayden could take it with him.

"Thank you, Ayden," he said opening the long glass windows behind them. Ayden nodded at Orion and flew out of the open window.

"Be careful."

# CHAPTER 22

"Get up, you're next!"

The iron bars rattled when the skeleton guard banged on the jail door startling Isa and Myran who was curled up on her lap. The guard grabbed Isa's arms pulling her out of the prison cave. Wanting to glance at her sister, Isa noticed that Safiya wasn't there. Not knowing where they were going, Isa was dragged alongside the guard through the castle until they stopped in front of a huge dark wooden door.

Light seeped from underneath the door and she could hear the voices of hundreds of people. Crowds seemed to be cheering to the sound of swords clashing and metal clanging. Then the sound of a screech and a body dropping to the ground made Isa realize where she was.

A roar of victory made the door rattle and the ground rumble.

Feeling the bony hands of the guard around her arm, Isa stepped into the arena when the guard opened the door. The colosseum looked similar to the one where she had fought General Adrastus in Atalia. She immediately saw blood stained on the sand before her. Isa lifted her hand to cover her eyes from the blinding light of the sun.

The cheers were coming from all sorts of dark creatures: goblins, orcs, ogres all from the Wastelands. Isa started walking towards the center of the fighting arena when she noticed above the stony wall was a booth where Maziar was sitting on a purple cushioned throne with Safiya next to her side. Looking in front of her, Isa suddenly saw who she would be fighting against. A putrid green troll holding an axe with his hands enjoying the praises from the crowd. As soon as Maziar made eye contact with Isa who was standing in the sandy arena, she held out her hands as the crowd went silent.

"My friends, my people!" She started. "I bring you a challenger for your champion. Before you, I present the Phantom!"

Except for her old General, Isa had not heard anyone else call her by her nom de guerre. The name she used while fighting the war in Endrancia. Glancing briefly at Safiya's emotionless face, Isa watched as the troll finally turned to face her. Taking a good look at him, Isa sized up her opponent, who only wore a chest plate of leather armor.

"Are you here to challenge my title?" The troll said in a deep voice trying to intimidate Isa. Surveying the arena, she looked at the edges of the arena where spears, axes, and all sorts of weapons were displayed.

Maziar smiled.

"Let the battle begin!" She yelled across the coliseum as the crowd cheered.

Waiting patiently, Isa watched as the troll charged at her. He swung his axe at her. Dodging it, Isa circled away and ran to the row of weapons. Analyzing her choices, Isa saw a staff propped up against the stone and a sword. The voice of Sir Alexander came flooding into her mind. *"A sword is for killing. And when you pick it up, you take that burden with you. You pay the price."*

Isa picked up a sword and ran to the opposite end of the arena facing the troll again. The yells of the crowd were deafening but Isa remained focused. Twirling the sword in her hand tasting the weight and feel, she steeled herself as the troll charged at her.

With a sudden move, Isa brought her sword up and stabbed the troll into his shoulder between the collarbone and neck killing him instantly. She landed on her feet, rolling before standing up behind him gracefully. Then she looked up at Maziar and Safiya. The coliseum was quiet until the crowd stood up cheering for Isa. Isa threw the bloody sword onto the ground with a clang and turned to leave the grounds.

Safiya clapped along happily.

⸻ ⬥ ⸻

*"Did you really kill the Crusher? We all talked about him,"* Myran started walking over to Isa before sitting down. Blinking slowly, Isa turned to the young dragon.

"I would rather not talk about what happened today. I did what I had to do to survive," she said, picking out sand grains from underneath her nails.

*Escape. Escape. Escape. I need to find a way to escape this prison. I need to scout every single corner of the castle.* She repeated in her mind.

*"Hey Isa, can I ask you a question?"* Myran asked from beside her.

"Yes, what's in your mind?" She asked softly looking at the young dragon as he distracted Isa from her thoughts.

*"It's about my age."* Myran paused his tail curling around his body. *"It's embarrassing, actually."*

*"I've been in here longer than everybody else. Maziar never lets me out. I may look young but I am actually three years old. I should be almost fully grown by now."*

"When I find a way to escape, I promise to take you with me to Atalia, Myran. You will be able to enjoy the sun and being outside," Isa added.

*"Really? Do you truly promise to take me with you?"* He looked up at her with big eyes making Isa chuckle.

"I'm not going to let you wither away in here. You will love living in Deval," she smiled at him winking.

Myran's wings flapped in happiness as he started jumping around the cave.

Watching him, Isa smiled.

It was clear to Isa that Queen Maziar had restricted his dragon's growth by preventing Myran from absorbing the sun's light. Isa wanted to help him and she planned to take him so he could grow to his full adult size.

Isa's plot and escape plan began that day.

---

Another day, another fight.

Isa knew that it was time for her to come forth and accept her new blood magic. She intended to use it at the fighting arena today. She needed to practice, get stronger, explore her new power and learn from it.

Looking at the pool of blood on the sand from the previous fight in the arena made Isa's hand tingled. The crowd cheered her name this time when Isa walked into the coliseum. Acknowledging the crowd, Isa started waving at them, which made them cheer louder. She knew that would make Maziar angry.

Isa turned around and was faced with another opponent.

This time a chimera which had the head and body of a lion and the tail had the head of a snake. The head roared and the tail hissed at her. Maziar gave the signal, then Isa charged against the creature and so did he. Swinging her sword with style, Isa managed to slice part of the lion's face when the creature jumped at her. The lion's head roared in pain in its eye. Looking down at the sword, Isa watched as the blood on the steel dripped down onto the sandy gravel.

As the chimera regained itself, Isa took the blood from her sword and covered her hand in it.

Running towards the chimera, Isa brutally decapitated the head of the snake. The chimera roared which gave Isa time to slide across the sand and slice its ankles. With a thump, the chimera was forced to the ground. Isa placed her bloody hand on the lion head to make an imprint. She could feel the heaviness in her hand and the heartbeats of the chimera.

The crowd remained silent in anticipation.

When Isa closed her fist, the chimera's head exploded in front of her.

A lot of blood covered her face and body. Instead of cheers, there were whispers among the crowd. Throwing the sword on the gravelly sand, Isa turned around walking away. All she could feel underneath her feet was the rumble of the arena caused by the roaring of the crowds. Meanwhile from the booth, Safiya was clapping and watching her sister walk out of the arena. Everyone saw what the Power of the Erythro could do.

⚬

Trying to get some sleep was very difficult for Isa because of the noises and clangs coming from the cages. She wished to be back in Atalia. She wished she could be with her friends. She wished to see Orion again. Her mind drifted to the last conversation they had together in the secret room. She was worried about him and his safety.

Isa wrapped her arms around herself thinking about Orion's embrace. He was kind and hadn't judged her once, he made her feel whole. He would be doing anything in his power to come and rescue her.

Isa closed her eyes and let out a sigh when Myran's curled up body pressed against her trying to keep her warm.

The sudden flap of wings and kack made Isa jump. She recognized that sound.

*"Isa! Isa! Are you there?"*

"Ayden?" She whispered looking around.

Ayden suddenly flew into view and managed to squeeze

through the iron bars. Flying into her arms, Isa embraced Ayden.

"Ayden! It's really you!" Isa said cuddling him as he leaned into her chest

"What's going on?" Safiya asked through the hole in the rock rubbing her eyes.

Isa turned to her and explained.

"Safiya, this is my friend Ayden. Ayden, this is my sister Safiya. Oh Ayden, I need to tell you so much about what I learned about my family, my new magic and what I learned from it today. I am happy you found me. Why are you here? You risked your life by coming here."

*"Isa, I'm here to bring you a message from Orion."* Ayden shook his head getting closer to Isa.

"A message?" She asked hesitantly, interlocking her hands making Safiya perk up.

Ayden lifted his leg up to show Isa the rolled-up piece of parchment paper wrapped in his talon. Grabbing it, Isa unraveled it quickly, leaning back to read it eagerly.

***My Isa,***

***I've been trying to find ways to rescue you. But it has been difficult. I plan to send my troops to the***

*border of Atalia to wait for you there and help you once you cross over the border from Zudora. It's the only way. Atalia can't risk declaring war right now, but I am trying everything in my power to get you back home with me.*

*I am working hard to be a good King. As good as my father was. My mother and I owe you our lives. You are very strong and brave. When I asked you to marry me, I wanted you to rule by my side.*

*Come back to me, Isa.*

*Orion*

Isa stayed silent, soaking in his words and making sure she had memorized them in her mind. *Orion was trying to find a way to save her.*

*"He's desperate to have you back home, Isa. But doing so, he could start a war,"* Ayden said as Isa turned to him nodding.

Finding a piece of wood from the edge of the cave, Isa passed it to Safiya and asked her to burn it. Isa knew she could use the ashes to write Orion back on the back of the paper. Safiya handed the ashes to Isa through the hole. Isa started writing back as quickly as she could.

**Orion,**

**I have an escape plan, please be patient. Princess Safiya is safe.**

**Stay strong for me. Be the King that Atalia needs right now. I'll be with you soon.**

**Isa**

She handed the paper back to Ayden.

"Don't come back here again. I can't have your death on my conscience," Isa said, leading Ayden to the iron bars. She looked down at him making sure he understood.

Ayden nodded.

*"I wanted to help you and make sure you were alive. Stay strong. Stay alert. Stay alive,"* the falcon told her.

"I will, I promise.

# CHAPTER 23

Having defeated every opponent that Queen Maziar had chosen to put in front of her, Isa discovered what her blood magic could do. It was versatile and unique. Her magic was growing stronger everyday. However, her energy seemed to slip away every time she spilled her own blood during the fights.

Winning every flight for Maziar's Kingdom gave Isa a bitter flavor though. She did not want to continue using her blood magic to kill. She did not want to be used by Maziar. Isa's constant inner struggles were weakening her inner strength. She couldn't focus.

As the skeleton guards dragged another dead body from the arena, Isa glanced over to see her sister Safiya, seated very pensive next to the Queen. Maziar, on the other hand, seemed extremely content relaxing against her lush chair crossing her leg enjoying the cheering of the crowd.

"Bring them in," Maziar commanded the guard. He bowed and walked away.

"What are you doing?" Safiya asked, confused and intrigued.

The Queen Maziar ignored her question and waved her hand.

Safiya saw a group of black minotaur's walking toward the booth to talk to the Queen. *What is happening? What is she planning to do?*

Their leader standing taller with gold rings around his horns and nostrils made eye contact with Maziar. They looked demonic like a nightmare that haunts even the bravest of people. Maziar was gesturing for them to come forward.

Maziar cleared her throat and talked to the leader. "I have a new product to sell. This is the Phantom from Atalia." Maziar smiled and then held out a hand gesturing to the fight to begin.

*Oh no. She is going to sell Isa. Why? She is her new champion.* Safiya tensed up trying to figure out what the Queen had in mind. Safiya's hands started heating up in anger. She could not let this happen. Isa was her sister and family. She desperately was trying to find a way to warm Isa.

The Queen continued, "She'll make a good wife or whatever you want to do with her." Maziar paused, popping a grape in her mouth. "She is not valuable to me anymore." Maziar continued.

"You did well, Maziar." His voice was deep and rugged. "I can see her markings. She has the *Power of the Erythro*. I understand that she is favored by the King of Atalia. And I am prepared to go to war to have her."

"Did you notice her blood magic? Isa is the last of the Bertocchi line. What more can you ask?" Maziar said, glancing at the creature beside her.

"The Phantom, your champion is of the Bertocchi family?" The minotaur hummed to himself.

"You have a deal. We will come to collect her tomorrow."

Maziar nodded, agreeing slowly as the minotaur stood up and left the coliseum.

Isa saw the minotaurs and was curious by the unexpected visitors the Queen had this morning. On the other hand, Isa noticed that something was bothering. Safiya's heart rate increased. She has to warn Isa before tomorrow and help her escape.

Queen Maziar saw Safiya's tension and said "If you tell Isa what you heard, I will take the children of the Kingdom and I will kill them all in front you. And if I hear anything about a possible escape, I will kill everyone."

Safiya was sad and silent.

⚬

"Since my last fight, I found out I can send crystalized projectiles of blood towards my opponent!"

*"You are incredible!"* The young dragon said, watching intently to Isa.

Isa kept the young dragon entertained with stories from her fights. During her free time in the cave, Isa started training the dragon. The most he could do was let out a small burst of flame from his mouth before it disintegrated. Isa was determined to escape and take her sister and the dragon with her. She would do it tonight. It was useless to wait any longer. She knew Orion's troops were waiting for her at the border.

Isa heard a skeleton guard drag Safiya by her arm and pushed her inside the cave. Safiya stayed silent on her pillowed floor for a while, frowning and refusing to say a word.

"Safiya, what is bothering you ?" Isa asked as peeked through the hole in the rock. Her sister seemed upset. *What did Maziar say to her?*

Sighing, Safiya finally turned to look at Isa.

"I need to tell you something very important. Just listen before it is too late. I am not sure if I mentioned this to you but our father told me about the Bertocchi heirloom that is locked beneath this castle." Isa furrowed her eyebrows.

*A family heirloom?*

"It's a blood gauntlet. It gives you the ability to control people through their blood without having to bleed them first. Your mother had it. I know where it is."

"Where is it?" Isa asked.

"It's underneath the castle and locked up. Maziar hasn't found it yet," Safiya said. "You will need to get it as soon as possible. You will need it to escape. I will stay behind so we don't raise any attention."

"I am not leaving without you. You're coming with me.

Come to Atalia with me. Orion and I will be your allies to help you reclaim the throne and overthrow Maziar," Isa remarked.

"I can't. This is my home, my people, Isa. I can't just abandon them," Safiya added rubbing her hands together.

Isa's heart panged against her chest.

"Listen to me, Safiya. Come with me and we will help you fight to liberate your kingdom from Queen Maziar," Isa continued. "You can't live here in fear for the rest of your days like this. Your people need you and once you're safe over the border Orion and I can help you," Isa smiled at her as she held out her hand through the hole.

"You can use your fire magic freely again without restriction," Isa added, trying to convince Safiya who seemed unsure.

"Isa, I have to tell you something else. The minotaurs today," She hesitated swallowing. She couldn't risk the lives of her people.

"Never mind."

"My lady is summoning you."

Isa followed the guard out of the cave.

She followed the guard as they walked into the cold and gloomy throne room. Maziar's emblem hung across the ashy wood beams of the roof that seemed to already be half burned. The skeleton guard stopped Isa in front of Maziar and walked away, disappearing.

"Queen Maziar, why am I here?"

Isa looked between Maziar and Safiya who refused to make eye contact with Isa.

"I summoned you here because I wanted to have the pleasure to tell you that I have sold you."

"Sold me to whom? Why?"

Maziar just laughed.

"You are my property. I can do whatever I want with you."

Isa was silent.

"I would even say I have been kind to you. I could have killed you the first day I brought you here and poisoned you the same way I poisoned the people of your villages.

Isa's eyes widened.

*Maziar is responsible for the black poison magic? The*

*dark magic that is spreading to the children now is Maziar's magic.*

Suddenly, black minotaurs burst through the doors. The leader spoke to Maziar. "We come to collect our property. Your payment is here." He said throwing a huge bag of gold at Maziar's feet.

"She is ready for you."

"You can't do this!" Isa yelled, panicking. "Orion will come and find me." Isa said.

They started pulling Isa away roughly while Isa tried resisting and turned back to face Maziar.

"He won't know where you are taken. Your little sister should have told you."

"You knew, Safiya?"

"I'm sorry." Safiya whispered.

Isa was silent.

"I know everything that happened in this castle. If your falcon ever comes back again looking for you, I will kill him on the spot.

Maziar stood up fully and waved at the minotaurs. At her signal, they started leading her away. As Isa struggled, she looked over her shoulder to Safiya who was in tears blaming herself and at Maziar who was walking back up to sit down on the throne.

"You will regret this, Maziar!"

"Will I? I see this as a success."

Before she could reply, Isa was knocked unconscious.

Being in a very dark room and blindfolded, Isa's senses seemed to heighten. She could hear the crackling of the torches and fast pace of her own breath. Her heart rate increased hearing the emptiness around her. Isa stayed calm and in silence to focus on her breathing.

Her silence was interrupted by the sound of hooves approaching her. Isa could smell the matted blood on the creature's fur in front of her. Her hands tingled trying to find the source but she couldn't see anything.

"Where am I? Who are you? " Isa asked. A ruff chuckle surrounded her as she turned towards the sound.

"Somewhere far away, but forgive my manners. My name is Tallon."

"I'm Isa-."

"It's an honor to have you here, Isa Bertocchi."

Hearing the creature walk around her chair, Isa stayed motionless.

"Our families were allies, you know. Best friends. It was a surprise to us when your family decided to join the light and betray us. The Bacia Clan was peaceful before the Bertocchi family came pillaging with their blood magic, they massacred my family in front of me. Some of us survived and we managed to escape to the wastelands."

"I found out recently that I am the last one of the Bertocchi and I have-." She was interrupted again.

"Do you think that changes anything? You think that's going to bring back my family?"

He let out a snort.

"I bought you for a reason only. I want you to fight for me and bring you back to the darkness where your family belongs."

The minotaur forcefully slammed a knife into her thigh making Isa scream in pain. Keeping the knife lodged in her leg, Isa tried to flinch away from it but he kept the steel lodged in her thigh. Isa felt the blood drenching her clothes. Cold drops mixed with her blood as the pulse of magic disappeared from her hands.

"If you don't agree to this, you will suffer for all eternity. I will weaken you until you say "yes"." He paused, coming back up to whisper right into Isa's face. His breath smelled of rotting meat.

"Get ready. Nothing will stop us."

Isa felt helpless.

Tallon dragged the tip of a knife across her skin. The creature stopped at the spot above her collarbone and started to slowly press the knife again. Feeling the immense pain, Isa tried not to make a sound.

The pain of the blade was too much for Isa to handle as she let out an ear-piercing scream.

# CHAPTER 24

With lack of food and limited water, Isa felt the pain of torture intensify tenfold. Her old wounds were scabbing up but there were so many new ones in her body. Isa's torturer was letting her slowly bleed out. Her blood magic was not strong in her anymore. However, Isa won't give up and she won't marry him.

The minotaur Tallon never let her sleep. He was determined to continue torturing Isa until she said yes. Isa had never felt this hopeless, being tied to a chair and not being able to move at all. She needed to stay alive and find a way to escape.

Being blindfolded made it even worse. Isa could not see the face of her captor. Tallon always was making sure to leave Isa in absolute silence. Tears had dried around her cheeks making the cloth around her eyes wet. Dried blood crusted around her mouth and her neck.

Isa seemed to cherish the moment of silence and peace when he is left alone. She closed her eyes and waited for nothing. She felt weak and suddenly she felt drifting herself into a complete darkness.

Surrounded by complete darkness, Isa slowly opened her eyes to a beautiful blue sky. Blinking in confusion, the fluffy white clouds moved gently across her vision. Opening and closing her eyes, Isa let the wind brush over her face. The wind calmed her as she took in the feeling of tranquility.

*Where am I? This is so nice and peaceful.*

Feeling the soft grass beneath her, Isa sat up with a sigh to see where she was. Furrowing her eyebrows, she found herself outside of the castle in Deval.

"Come and look!"

Isa turned around as the wind blew her long wavy dark hair into her face. Moving it away, she was met with a little girl in front of her holding up a white flower for her to take.

Isa swallowed trying to regain her voice watching the child before her.

"What a beautiful flower." Isa smiled as she accepted

the flower from the child.

The child had big blue eyes with curly dark brown hair and she looked to be barely five years old.

"But not as beautiful as you are mommy." Isa grinned watching the child.

Leaning against her hand, Isa could smell the flower. Touching the green grass, she let the breeze blow her hair around. She wanted this moment to last as long as it possibly could. Isa continued watching the small child play in the grass as the clouds passed through the breeze and the sun warmed her skin.

Suddenly Orion came into her view and ran to the child picking her up twirling her around in his arms making her squeal in happiness.

"Daddy, daddy! Put me down!"

"Orion?" Isa whispered standing up in surprise.

Whispering to the child, Orion put the child down on the ground before he came to Isa.

"I'm dreaming, aren't I?" She whispered.

"Yes, you are and so am I. I've been waiting for you."

Isa ran to Orion embracing him and clinging onto him. Tears fell down her eyes. "You are here. You came for me."

Orion pulled back and grasped her face like it was the last time he would ever see her.

"Orion, I'm sorry-. I-," Isa started.

Orion kissed the side of her head slowly closing his eyes. They stayed in each other's arms for a long time before they both leaned back. Isa moved her hands to Orion's face stroking his cheeks with the back of her hand.

"When I asked you to marry me, something happened and we connected with each other."

Isa sighed sadly looking down at the grass below them.

"Orion, Maziar sold me to the minotaurs. I have no clue where I am."

Orion was silent as his eyes widened more in shock, his jaw clenching.

"Orion, I am dying. I'm so sorry." Isa whispered.

"No, don't say that." He said. "I will find you."

Then, Isa looked down at her fingers seeing them slowly disappearing.

"What's happening, Orion?" She looked up at him in shock as he stepped towards her grabbing her hands again grounding her.

"You're waking up."

Chest heaving, Isa shook her head furiously.

"The minotaur Tallon from the Bacia Clan is bleeding me slowly and weakening me. He's using poison to stop me from using my own blood magic." Tears burned behind her eyes in thought of waking up as Isa's arms fully disappeared.

Orion nodded trying to keep her calm.

"Stay strong, Isa."

Orion nodded again and then with Isa's face in his hands, he pulled her into him.

Shaking, Isa woke up with a gasp and was met with darkness again. All she could hear was the slow breaths of Tallon against her face.

"I can't have you pass out on me? You have to stay awake my dear." His rancid breath tickling the side of her face.

Isa screamed as another knife plunged into her body making her shake and convulse.

⸺◆⸺

Safiya paced back and forth in her own cave. *I should not have betrayed her. She is my family. How could I do this to her? Where could she be? I will ask my spies in the castle to follow the minotaurs next time they are visiting Maziar.*

"Guards, guards! I request to see Queen Maziar," Princess Safiya said in a commanding voice.

And before she knew it, Safiya was escorted by one of the skeleton guards to the throne room. Maziar was waiting for her.

"Princess Safiya! Is there anything I can do for you today? You deserve to be rewarded for your loyalty."

"Queen Maziar, I think my people and your supporters need a new champion for the fights now that my sister Isa is gone."

"Clever girl. Good thinking. Are you planning to be in the fights to replace your sister?"

Queen Maziar pressed a hand on Safiya's shoulder.

"No, not me. I was thinking of Myran. He is a rare dragon and everybody will come to see him in a fight. The spectators will pay a higher price to see him in action. He needs to start training outside."

"Hmmmm. Let me think. He is young at the moment but could become strong in a few months. And he could become loyal to me as well."

Safiya kept her face neutral as she was escorted back to

her prison.

There, Myran shook in terror but Safiya reassured him that afternoon that many changes would happen soon.

He just needed to trust her.

# CHAPTER 25

Quinn heard the hooves of a horse before he saw Orion and Nova rushing onto their property. Reaching for the reins, Quinn helped the new King.

"King Orion, your majesty. A pleasure to have you here." Quinn said with furrowed eyebrows while Orion was dismounting Nova. Wiping his forehead, Orion caught his breath before addressing him.

"Quinn, I would like to see Amarantha. Where is she?" Orion asked once he landed on his feet. Before Quinn could answer, the Princess peaked around the corner of the door looking worried having heard the commotion.

"Orion? What are you doing here?" She asked, wiping her hands on her apron and stepping towards them. Quinn took Nova to the stable walking past Amarantha.

Walking up to him, Amarantha looked at him worried. "Are you alright? I am happy for your visit, your highness.

I heard that Isa was taken."

He interrupted Amarantha. "Yes, she has been captured."

"Can I come in and talk inside?"

As they both walked into the stone cottage, Orion took a heavy seat at their dining table wiping his face from more grime and sweat still on his skin.

"Orion, would you like some water to drink?" Quinn asked as Orion looked up and sadly grinned up at him.

"Yes, water please."

Quinn nodded going into the kitchen. Amarantha sat down opposite Orion as he looked around the house confused by how empty the house was.

"Where's Beth?" He asked. Amarantha sat silent and waited until Quinn returned, handing Orion some water before turning back to him.

"They went to see a plot of land near here for farming and to buy some livestock." She explained.

Orion nodded understanding. As he was about to open his mouth to begin explaining his sudden arrival, a baby started crying in the room next to them.

Sighing, Amarantha stood up and walked to the room.

Orion heard shushing and Amarantha walked back carrying a newborn baby in her arms. Amarantha soothed the infant as Orion's eyes widened looking between the baby and Amarantha.

Amarantha sat down, Quinn placed a hand on her shoulder while she was caressing the baby's cheeks. The baby has Amarantha's darker skin and straight black hair, but she had Quinn's hazel green eyes. A beautiful child, the best of Atalian and Endrancian blood.

"Congratulations to both of you." Orion said, making the young parents look up at him and smile.

"Thank you, your highness. Her name is Lilly." Quinn said.

"Do you mind if I have a word with Orion, please." Amarantha said, turning serious.

"Sure. Of course," Quinn said before placing a kiss to her lips leaving them alone.

"Isa has been captured by Maziar? The Queen in Zudora?" Amarantha asked.

He nodded and shared with her what had happened the evening of the Ball. Orion swallowed trying not to break down.

"Isa sacrificed herself to protect me and Atalia. To protect all of us. I asked her to marry me to rule by my side but she was taken. We had only recently found out she was the last of the Bertocchi family." Orion finished as he looked down at the wood table picking at his fingers.

Orion placed his elbows on the table letting his emotions get the best of him. As the sniffles turned into sobs, Amarantha stood up and walked around to Orion placing a comforting hand on his shoulder. Rubbing his back, Amarantha looked down at her friend completely breaking down in front of her.

"So sorry about your father and Isa, Orion."

Orion interrupted her. "Amarantha, I came here today to ask for your help." he said looking back up at her as she nodded hearing him.

Sighing, Orion spoke. "I know this will sound strange but I had a dream and Isa came to me to tell me that Queen Maziar sold Isa to the minotaurs. She is being held hostage by a Tallon from the Bacia Clan. Do you know anything about this clan."

Amarantha's eyes immediately widened. Seeing this Orion looked up at her confused.

"The Bacia clan is an old clan of minotaurs from across the continent. They were known to be merciless and evil. A couple hundred years ago, they killed one of Endrancia's most beloved Kings. As it is mentioned in our records, it was a brutal assassination, so much so that everyone feared to go outside the kingdom. They were responsible for the spread of dark magic in Endrancia."

"You said that Isa's family name is Bertocchi?" Amarantha asked.

Orion nodded.

"The Bertocchi family rescued the Endrancian Royal Family that were held hostage by the Bacia clan. This family, with their blood magic, started hunting down the clan of minotaurs and saved our royal family in Endrancia. Without them, my family wouldn't be ruling Endrancia today." Amarantha said.

"And Isa saved me when I was in the forest. The Bertocchi family has proven again to have been benefactors to the Rafiq family.

"But what of Isa being the true heir of the Zudoran throne?"

Amarantha nodded thinking more. "What was Isa's

mothers name?"

"Rosa Bertocchi."

Amarantha was silent as she looked down at the ground, her eyes moving back and forth in thought.

"What is it?" Orion asked worriedly.

"Isa's great-grandmother was Shakeela Rafiq. Shakeela Rafiq, the animal tamer."

Orion's eyes widened again.

"So, you're saying that-," Orion started as he slowly looked up at Amarantha to see her nodding along.

"Her great-grandmother was the one who passed down the ability to talk to animals and is my great-grandfather's sister. We are connected."

"Orion, Isa is the descendant of three major households. The Bertocchi's and the Von Brandt's mainly, but also my own house, the Rafiq's. Once you marry her, the Dawn Monarchy will also be added to that list." Amarantha paused.

"I will reach out to my father. The Endrancian Kingdom needs to help rescue Isa Bertocchi. The world is changing around us and you need more allies against the Bacia clan."

"Thank you, Amarantha." Orion took her hand and pressed it against his forehead. She waved him off, making him release her hand.

---

The door burst open with a crash as Tallon pounded towards Isa where she sat motionless, slowly breathing. Her head hung down weakly as she carefully lifted her head up hearing him trying hard to speak. Swallowing, she made sure her mouth was wet enough to talk.

Angrily, Tallon finally ripped the blindfold off of Isa's eyes as she groaned and hissed, closing her eyes. The light from the torches was too much after being blindfolded for so long.

Isa blinked rapidly, the harsh image of the minotaur finally came into her eyesight. She could finally see him for the first time and look him in the eyes.

"My spies tell me there are troops leaving the castle of Atalia?"

Isa took a deep breath pausing as her eyes adjusted.

"How did you send a message?"

Tallon threatened Isa with a knife to her jaw. "Tell me

how!"

Isa stayed silent and slowly turned her head to spit at the ground. Looking up at the minotaur again, steam came out of his nostrils. Looking up at him, Isa gritted her teeth, biting her lip trying not to show any weakness.

"I don't know!"

Seeing her body shake, Tallon waved her off as he walked to the door of the room, opening it then leaning through it.

"Double the guards! Double everything! I don't want my weapon to be taken away from me!" He shouted for the guards to follow his orders.

Isa lifted her chin as she whispered even though she didn't believe in her own words.

"I will never surrender. This is not the end."

# CHAPTER 26

I sa lost track of time in her torture chamber. Her body wasn't healing as quickly as it should have. Dried blood, scabs, grime, and bruises covered her weak body. Her scalp felt itchy and greasy as she resisted the urge to move in fear of causing more pain. Isa's thoughts were empty, her body shivering against the cold floor. The crackling of the torches was the only thing keeping her company in the cold and empty stone room.

An occasional rumble on the ceiling dropped some dirt and dust onto Isa. Her eyes moved slightly watching the debris, but then she closed them trying to get some sleep and regain before Tallon came back. He had taken her chair away and instead left her on the dirty and wet stone floor. He made sure to weaken Isa enough so that she would not run away or fight him back. Ultimately, Tallon will keep waiting until Isa says yes and marry him.

Her chest started moving up and down slowly. She was waiting for her body to give out.

Suddenly, the rumble happened again and the vibration of the floor jolted her body. Opening her eyes, she heard quick footsteps tapped against the stone. Isa's heart spiked dreading to have Tallon come back. Then, she heard heavy thuds against the walls and floor.

"Isa! Where are you?"

Letting out a breath, Isa thought that she was hallucinating. *This is just another dream. This time I don't want to wake up.* Isa's eyes fluttered with unshed tears.

The door flew open and someone burst through the door and immediately saw Isa on the floor gasping.

"Isa! Isa! It's me Safiya"

Recognizing her sister's voice, Isa weakly turned her head slowly seeing her. Rushing towards Isa and kneeling down, Safiya reached out to gently lift Isa's head. Her neck cracked as Safiya's warm hands gave Isa some strength.

"Safiya? It's you!" Isa whispered, her voice coarse. Looking at her sister, tears built up behind her eyes and a sense of relief flooded her body.

"Damn, you don't look so good, Isa." Safiya said, cradling her head.

Isa smiled trying not to wince. "I couldn't clean up for your arrival."

Safiya chuckled while turning her head back to Isa's face. Sweat coated the lining of her light brown hair, which was up in a ponytail showing off the flame marking on her neck and she wasn't wearing her usual royal garb.

Finally seeing Safiya face to face, Isa noticed her light yellow amber eyes and freckles sprinkled across her cheeks and nose. Her features were more regal, sharper than her own.

"Your sarcasm is always well-timed." Safiya joked, her eyes misting slightly.

"At least I have some wit about me." Isa coughed before fully registering that her sister was with her.

"But, how did you find me?" Isa gasped.

"The torches told me. One of my spies followed the minotaur when he came to see Maziar the other day. Tallon seemed very unhappy."

Isa nodded, not having enough energy to ask for a full explanation. Seeing Safiya by herself, Isa looked around the room curiously.

"How did you manage to get in? Where's Myran?" At her question, Safiya grinned at her getting excited.

"I convinced Maziar to train Myran for the fights since she needed a new champion. When he was exposed to the outside light, Myran started growing rapidly. He's now fortified the castle and he is distracting Maziar while I escaped."

Isa nodded again giving a slight grin as she let out a breath relaxing in Safiya's arms.

"How did you manage to escape?" Isa asked, looking up at Safiya's eyes.

Smiling, Safiya answered knowing that Isa was going to ask that question.

"Well, I was helped by some of your devoted admirers from the fights. They would do anything to have you back in the arena, you know. " She said, smiling and turning her head towards the door.

"I will tell you more later. We need to get you out of here and take you over the border." Safiya chuckled as they started towards the open door.

Stumbling and tripping over her own feet, Isa tried not

to make it any harder for her sister. They stepped across the threshold of the chamber room that had kept Isa isolated.

"What happened to Tallon?" Isa asked as they managed to pick up the pace and turned to the left going into a lit-up stone hallway.

As they came to another corridor, a minotaur came bounding towards them with an axe.

"He is just behind us. Let's hurry up."

Safiya stopped and managed to wave the fire from the torches towards Tallon. The fire obeyed, sending a stream of fire towards the minotaur, who screamed from being burned alive.

Engulfed in flame, Tallon started running away. It all happened so quickly that Isa blinked trying to remain conscious as the walls started to blur.

Isa was impressed by the display of fire magic from her sister.

While Safiya kept burning and spearing more skeleton guards and minotaurs along the way, Isa kept glancing back and tried to keep up. Her body was so weak. Isa's blood magic was melting away. Safiya placed a hand on Isa which made her blink and breathe out in relief again.

A spark of energy seemed to flow through her body when her sister touched her shoulder. Stumbling, Isa placed one foot in front of the other as they reached a stone staircase.

"Safiya, where are we?" Isa asked as another rumble sounded above them. More debris and dust flew to the floor as they all coughed. That's when they knew they were close to the ground level.

"We are still in Zudora." Safiya said matter of fact.

Isa's eyes widened at her comment.

"Tallon, the minotaur was smart enough to not bring you to his hometown in fear that you may kill them all." she chuckled, but Isa was still in shock.

"Maziar gave him a torture chamber for him to use. You've been here the whole time." Safiya nodded letting out a breath.

As they continued up the staircase, they finally reached a huge iron bolted door that was unlocked. Releasing Isa, Safiya ran to the door and grunted, pushing it open slowly. Sunlight and fresh air poured into Isa's face. She took a deep breath.

"Finally free."

They walked past the iron door and into the familiar hallways of the castle but Isa couldn't ignore the searing heat of fire. Turning to the side as the girls pressed on, the yellow and orange flames rose around the walls of stone like ivy and surrounded the edges of the columns preventing anybody from getting in. Ash and rubble covered the ground around them as smoke rose in the banisters above them like gray storm clouds.

Hearing screams from behind the wall of fire, Isa looked around.

"We can't leave without my mother's gauntlet!" Isa asked, but Safiya shook her head as they kept trying to hurry.

"No, it's too risky. But it is hidden in a safe underground chamber. For now ,we have to get out of here as soon as possible. " Safiya urged, dodging through the flames.

They heard more roars of destruction. As they rounded another corner, Isa saw the image of a dragon with his wings outspread, sending streams of fire from his mouth blocking the entrance into the castle. Other creatures from the cages next to him defending the castle. It was an impressive display. Isa was mesmerized with Myran's adult body.

"Come on Isa. Myran will fly us out of here." Safiya said as they stopped behind Myran.

The ground rumbled beneath them. The heat of the fire pushed hot air around them. Sweat covered all of their skin.

The dragon turned his head around and saw the girls behind him.

*"Isa? You are alive."*

The fully grown white scaled dragon stepped towards them as the other creatures continued defending the castle.

*"I can only hold off Maziar for so long. Here, let me carry you,"* he said crouching down to the floor. Isa nodded and Safiya helped her mount Isa onto Myran. Once Isa was settled on his scales, she grabbed onto the horns on his back for stability when Safiya started pointing towards the exit.

"Let's go, this way!" Safiya said.

Seeing the dry spring grasses blended with the ash from

the flames, Isa tried not to pass out. Once they were a safe distance outside the castle, the creatures defending the entrance followed them into the forest for safety.

Stopping, Safiya, Isa and Myran turned their heads to look back at the castle. Black poured out from the castle as rock and stone fell down on itself like a rockslide. The flames were dying down but the damage was done. The smell of smoke and burning wood filled Isa's nose. The castle will become a ruin very soon.

Isa wanted all evidence of what had gone down in that castle to be destroyed. With fire comes the ashes of re-birth.

Fire cleanses.

Isa wanted her sister Safiya to have a kingdom without the traces of Maziar's destruction and wrath. A new kingdom for her sister and Zudora. This kingdom did not feel like home for Isa. This kingdom was home to Safiya.

Watching more of the destruction, Isa swallowed as Safiya waited patiently before Isa glanced at her. Taking a deep breath of fresh air, Isa stood up tall on top of Myran.

"Safiya, your people deserve a new kingdom to rebuild. We are finally liberating everyone." Isa stated.

Eyes widening, Safiya looked at her older sister shocked before realizing what she meant. Lifting her hands towards the castle, Safiya looked back up at her older sister, waiting for Isa's command ready to jump into action. Glancing down at her from a top Myran, Isa nodded before turning back up at the castle.

"Burn it to the ground. Leave nothing but ashes." Isa pronounced. Safiya nodded.

Slowly, the flames that had destroyed the castle rose up again like a bonfire engulfing the entirety of the castle.

⸺◆⸺

"My King, we have news from Zudora!"

A messenger ran towards Orion. He was huddled over a makeshift map of his troops across the Zudoran-Atalian border. Looking up in full navy blue and silver plated Atalian battle armor and chainmail, Orion stood up fully watching him carefully.

"What is it?" Orion asked as Ayden ruffled his feathers on top of his shoulder. Sweating, the messenger panted regaining his breath.

"There's been a riot at the castle. Reports are coming

in that a dragon has taken over the Castle of Fyre and smoke can be seen over the horizon. The dragon and other creatures have seized the castle."

Orion looked at him confused waiting for more information. The messenger nodded slowly at him as Orion's eyes widened in understanding.

"Our scouts from Zudora are saying they saw their Princess Safiya burn down the castle and she wasn't alone," the messenger said.

"Thank you, Adam." Orion excused the messenger. He bowed and turned around to leave the tent.

Orion glanced towards the falcon on his shoulder. Ayden knew what to do as he nodded and leapt into the air flying out between the curtains. Once the falcon was gone, Orion then looked at everyone standing before him still in the tent.

"Send reinforcements and healers to help with the refugees from Fyre. Lieutenant Carya, assemble a small team, we are going to the border now. Everybody else, prepare for a possible attack from Maziar," Orion commanded.

"Yes, your Majesty!"

After they all bowed to him and rushed outside, Orion closed his eyes and stayed in silence. He gave himself a second of peace before he too stepped outside his tent. Everywhere he looked throughout the camp, his army was busy preparing horses and sharpening weapons.

As he passed by, soldiers bowed towards Orion.

Orion kept strong for his people, for Atalia's allies and for Isa. Feeling a sense of relief in his chest, he hoped that Isa was nearby.

Once he reached the edge of the camp, a squire walked up to Orion bowing his head. He handed the King his ancestral light bow as he accepted it with a nod. Holding the weapon secure in his hand and making sure his arm guard and finger-guard were in place, Orion stopped as he looked up over the top of the trees.

"My King? Ready to go?" Lieutenant Carya asked, already on horseback with soldiers behind him. Looking up towards him, Orion nodded as another squire came up to him holding Nova's reins.

"Let's go," Orion said, stepping around to mount Nova before he thanked the squire taking a deep breath calming his racing heart.

Grabbing the reins, he stepped into the stirrups quickly mounting Nova before taking off into the forest with the bow in his hand ready for anything that may stop him from getting Isa back.

⚬

They kept flying down towards the small green hill when Safiya pointed at a clearing. Myran was getting closer to the border.

"We're almost there, Isa!" Safiya shouted.

Isa let out a breath of relief.

An arrow came flying and caught Isa in the arm. Grabbing her arm, Isa was thrown off Myran as she landed rolling onto the ground.

"No!"

"*Isa!*" Myran shouted, stopping as well.

As Isa recovered trying to sit up, she watched when Tallon, the minotaur approached her and started circling them. His hooves pounded against the ground as she could only watch.

Then a large figure shadowed over Isa. She looked up to see white scales. Growling, Myran stepped over to protect

Isa's body. Panting, she glared at the minotaur trying to stand up. The grass below her was stained red from her blood.

Suddenly, Safiya blocked her line of vision. Legs spread wide Safiya was ready to defend her older sister from an attack. With Safiya's fists in flames and Myran standing above her, they all watched the minotaur's snort at them unsheathing his own weapons.

"Princess, I will spare you if you give us back what's rightfully mine. My weapon, my pawn in this world," he said, opening a hoofed arm towards her in invitation.

"Never!" Safiya yelled bigger flames erupting from her hands as Myran growled again above Isa.

The minotaur didn't take kindly to her rejection as he pulled out an axe roaring at them. Nostrils flared, the minotaur pawed at the ground about to charge against Safiya, Myran, and Isa. But before the minotaur took another step, a high screech thrill followed by a thud was heard. Tallon's face went blank as his arms suddenly slumped down, dropping his axe.

He stood frozen watching the tip of a glowing white arrow penetrate his chest. The minotaur's black eyes rolled back into his head as his fur drained of color. His body swayed before falling forward and landing on the ground with a thump.

From behind stood Orion with his bow in hand ready to fire more white arrows.

He was here.

His light seemed to almost blind Isa as the darkness and poison within her body flew out. Unable to fight the urge, Isa bent over and hurled what looked like black goo from inside of her.

In fear of seeing the Atalian army coming closer, the other minotaurs grabbed their leader's body and fled back into the forest.

"Orion?" Isa whispered, watching as he slowly lowered the bow. Atalian soldiers rushed to Safiya, and Isa. The ache in her chest magnified, but a shred of doubt climbed into her head.

*Maybe this is a dream and I am still trapped by Tallon. He couldn't be here before me. What if this is part of his new way of torturing me?*

With her head.

With her mind.

As her mind tried to come up with an explanation, Isa's body couldn't take it anymore. She slumped down onto her back as stinging pain exploded all around her. Her hands and body shook as her chest heaved, breathing irregularly as sweat flowed from her skin.

Hearing Isa's convulse reaction, Safiya turned around confused as her eyes widened kneeling down next to Isa.

"Oh no. Stay awake Isa please! Breathe! She's going into shock!" Safiya called out behind her while Isa continued hyperventilating. Her vision blurred.

Voices merged together around Isa as a warm hand against her forehead calmed her mind. Head slumping against the grass, she fell back into a complete darkness.

Isa was not scared anymore.

It was not agony or pain. It was a different feeling alto-gether.

Hope.

## END OF BOOK ONE

*The Royal Atalian Chronicles*
*Book One of the Account of the 10th Reigning King and*
*Queen of Atalia*

## *Acknowledgments*

This book came to fruition one night after watching the CW Reign show and thinking 'What if Mary was a special forces soldier?' And the story pretty much wrote itself. So thank you to this show for inspiring Isa, Orion, and my story. And thanks to the actors for being the inspiration for my characters.

Thank you to my parents especially to my mom for reading early drafts of this book, editing, suggesting more details, and for always being there for me throughout all my life. I wouldn't be where I am without you.

Thank you to BookTok for being such a great community and for all of the great people that have I befriended, especially to BexGil for beta reading, always engaging, and supporting my novel to the fullest. This book wouldn't have been possible without all the guidance and kindness everyone has shown me.

And a very special thanks to you.

This wouldn't have been possible without you. Thank you for supporting me by reading this book and for taking the time to read Isa and Orion's journey. I can't believe you've made it this far! I couldn't have been happier and prouder.

Keep believing and never stop fighting for what is right no matter the cost, you will prevail.

Born in Upstate New York to an English father and Argentinian mother, Isabella grew up in California before moving to Colorado for university. With a BSc in Animal Sciences and a MSc in Applied Animal Welfare, Isabella has traveled and lived in many countries including Thailand, Costa Rica, and Scotland to pursue her animal passion. Since she was a little girl, she has fantasized about far-off worlds and started writing since she was able to. She currently lives in Arizona and spends her days playing her flute, reading, and competing in 3-day Eventing. *The Kingdom She Lost* is her debut novel.

Connect Online

@isabellawellsauthor

***Pronunciation Guide***

Isa: EE-sa

Orion: Oh-rye-un

Adrastus: Ad-ras-tus

Maziar: Ma-zee-ar

Safiya: Saf-ee-yah

Myran: My-run

Ayden: Like the name Aiden

Fyre: Fie-ray

Atalia: Ah-ta-lee-ah

Zudora: Zoo-door-ah

# THE
# LOST HEIR
# OF
# BLOOD

A NOVEL

BOOK TWO
THE ATALIAN CHRONICLES

S hivering under the light of a cell, Isa felt the cool paste that Najia was applying to her back while staying in her crouched position. It had been a week since Isa had been thrown into this new prison cell with some of her battle buddies from the garrison after enduring heavy torture. Isa only accepted the help of the prison doctor Najia's.

"Did you give away any information?" Najia asked.

At first Najia knew Isa would be silent so the doctor kept applying the healing paste as Isa's short dark curls fanned over her dark face. Isa let out another shiver before shaking her head.

"No." she whispered before letting out a dry cough wincing. Isa's voice was still sore and hoarse from her screams the week before.

Since they were the only two women in the prison,

Najia hoped that Isa saw her as a friend rather than an enemy. Sighing, Najia kept working pushing her curls away with her elbow. They were silent as the doctor finished spreading the paste and then put the bandage on Isa's back. Having lived and grown up in Endrancia her whole life, Najia hated what her people were doing to the Atalian's soldiers. She had seen her fair share of injuries in this prison.

Najia wanted to help them in any way she could, even if it meant being there for them as a friendly face. She too was trapped in that underground prison in her own way.

"You are a survivor; you will get out of here." Najia said, reassuring Isa. The doctor's fingers, covered in the red culture markings of Endrancia.

Isa stayed silent.

Najia sighed again before going around to face her. Hearing her movement, Isa lifted her head up with her arms wrapped around her body. Najia's dark black eyes searched hers.

"You've survived this far. You will live to tell the story." Najia said but continued.

Isa looked at her in disbelief. Najia knew what it must

look like, she had come out of a torturing situation and was still healing from the hands of her people.

"We will all get out of here." Daniel, a tall fit and muscular soldier from Isa's garrison, spoke up, giving her a thumbs up leaning against the dirty wet wall.

Isa weakly grinned up at him before turning back to Najia.

"Isa, hope and believe. I know it. I know it down here . . . in my gut." Najia smiled.

"You do not deserve to be locked up in here. Nobody does. But I know, you are going to do great things. You will not rot in this place; I won't let that happen." Najia added while brushing some long dark greasy hair away from Isa's dirty face.

Najia sat next to Isa. Leaning their heads against the damp stone of the cell, they were silent listening to the drips of water. Isa closed her eyes trying to get some rest. More droplets of water rang around them until Najia lifted her head.

Isa looked down at a rat that was roaming in the cell. The rat seemed to be focused on Isa as she nodded.

"Wait," Najia paused slowly, acknowledging what she

had seen. "You can talk to animals?"

Isa nodded at Najia's question.

"She was in the cavalry. Then she was promoted straight to the special forces because of her ability." Sam, another soldier, added grinning from the dark corner of the cell. The gears started to turn in Najia's head before Isa's eyes widened, lifting her body off of the wall.

"I have an idea." The doctor added.

Watching her, Isa made a face when she lifted an eyebrow at the doctor.

"Why don't you use your gift to escape?"

Isa was silent before another one of her team spoke up.

"The doctor has a point," Vernon said deeply from beside Daniel as they both nodded in agreement looking at each other.

Thinking about it, Isa stayed quiet. *I can talk to animals willing to scout out the area of the prison so I can get an accurate outline of the prison. How many officers are guarding the entrance?*

"It could work," Isa whispered as Najia nodded beside her. Then, Isa pushed herself off of the wall and onto her bruised smudged knees. The damp stone floor was covered in enough dirt and soil that Isa started to wipe the floor making a clean slate. The three soldiers and Najia stopped talking. Using her finger, Isa sketched an outline of what she knew of this prison before she started to examine her work.

"Here's what I know." Isa started to explain her possible plan.

With the sudden burst of energy, the soldiers started to plan their escape. They would get out of that underground prison. Isa was determined to save her whole team and take them back to Atalia including Najia.

*General Adrastus will send a rescue team that can meet at the border. I am sure he will save us all.* Isa thought.

They would all be free soon.

Najia grinned while Isa's eyes filled with hope.